I Love You, Julie

I LOVE YOU, JULIE

DAISY THOMSON

THORNDIKE
CHIVERS

This Large Print edition is published by Thorndike Press, Waterville, Maine, USA and by BBC Audiobooks Ltd, Bath, England.

Thorndike Press is an imprint of Thomson Gale, a part of The Thomson Corporation.

Thorndike is a trademark and used herein under license.

LIBRARY OF CONGRESS CATALOGING-IN-PUBLICATION DATA

Thomson, Daisy Hicks.
  I love you, Julie / by Daisy Thomson.
    p. cm. — (Thorndike Press large print Candlelight)
  ISBN-13: 978-0-7862-9468-8 (alk. paper)
  ISBN-10: 0-7862-9468-X (alk. paper)
  1. Large type books. I. Title.
  PR6070.H676I3 2007
  823'.914—dc22
                    2007002866

BRITISH LIBRARY CATALOGUING-IN-PUBLICATION DATA AVAILABLE

Published in 2007 in the U.S. by arrangement with Robert Hale Limited.
Published in 2007 in the U.K. by arrangement with Robert Hale Limited.

U.K. Hardcover: 978 1 405 64032 9 (Chivers Large Print)
U.K. Softcover: 978 1 405 64033 6 (Camden Large Print)

Printed in the United States of America on permanent paper
10 9 8 7 6 5 4 3 2 1

I LOVE YOU, JULIE

ONE

"I think we have gone over everything pretty thoroughly, don't you, Miss Gilbert?"

Murray Sheil ticked off the final items he had noted on the pad in front of him, and glanced inquiringly at me across the leather-topped desk.

"I have explained, as best I can, what Mrs. Briarton expects of you. I have told you about the hours of work, and the amount of free time you will have," he ticked the items off a second time, as if he wanted to be doubly sure he had missed nothing out.

"I have told you you can have the use of the family car whenever you want it, and I have told you the salary that goes with the job," he smiled at me, "but is there anything else you would like me to elaborate on?"

"Well, yes!" I smiled back at him. "You haven't told me the date on which I am expected to start work!"

"Ah! So you have decided to accept the

post!" exclaimed the young lawyer, a look of relief crossing his face. "I am so glad!"

He shook his head.

"The other two women I interviewed this morning decided against it. They didn't like the idea of living so far from civilisation, as they both put it!"

"Ardcraig is hardly the back of beyond!" I exclaimed. "I looked it up on the map. It can only be about an hour's fast drive from the county town.

"No," I told him, "I'm not worried about the isolation. What I am a bit doubtful about is Mrs. Briarton's age. Don't you think she might consider me too young for the job? I would have thought she would prefer someone more mature, someone in her forties or fifties."

Murray Sheil shook his head once more, and the way he continued to appraise me, with his attractive dark eyes, made me understand why the young secretary who had ushered me into his private office some twenty minutes earlier, had looked at him with such a starry-eyed gaze.

"Mrs. Briarton knew how old you were when she included your name in the short list of 'possibles' she asked me to interview for her," he told me. "In any case, apart from the fact that you have the necessary

8

qualifications, she told me she rather liked the idea of having a young person in the household, and she would have chosen you herself straightaway, but her innate caution made her decide to get another opinion, in case, as she put it, at a personal interview with an unprejudiced person, like me, you might prove not to have the kind of temperament with which she could get along."

"So temperamentally," I smiled at him, "I take it I have also passed the test?"

Sheil shuffled the papers on his desk into a neat pile.

"Mrs. Briarton, like her late husband, Brigadier Briarton, relies implicitly on my judgment when it comes to business matters. She knows I understand her, and if I say you are right for her, she will accept my decision.

"There is one thing, however, that worries me," he frowned, and pushed his chair back from the desk, to examine me critically once again, his gaze lingering appreciatively on the expensive fur hat which hugged my head, the smart, fine wool suit, the neckline adorned with a casually knotted silk square under the elegant fur trimmed coat which I had unbuttoned when sitting down to face him across his desk.

"You don't seem the type of woman who

is used to the life of a small rural community. I am not quite sure if you would settle in a remote house, in a remote Highland village for several months, with only an old lady of eighty, and her staff for company.

"In all fairness, I must point out the drawbacks. There are no cinemas, no theatres, no discos for miles around. Very little social life unless," for a moment a scowl replaced the frown, "you enjoy outdoor sports. The Hardys are trying to set up a Sports Complex in the area. Skiing, sailing, sea fishing, pony trekking, that sort of thing. The centre is about a couple of miles north of Ardcraig village, which would make it about eight or so miles from Matfield House.

"Then, too, the road between Matfield and the village can be blocked by snow sweeping down the mountains at this time of year, or, where it runs alongside the loch itself, on the borders of the Matfield estate, it can be inundated by high tides or stormy seas at any time of the year, so you could be marooned for days!

"Yes, it is only fair for me to warn you that Matfield might prove to be much more isolated than you imagine."

I laughed.

"Mr. Sheil, surely you are not trying to

talk me out of taking the job at this late stage?" I cocked my head at him.

"Miss Gilbert," he retorted, "believe me, nothing would please me more than to have you accept it. I know Mrs. Briarton will like you. I myself would feel happy to know that my old friend has someone like you with her, and yet, I have to think of you too."

He tapped the papers on the desk in front of him.

"Having read about your background, of the interesting cosmopolitan life you have led as a roving reporter, and as a woman's magazine fashion editor, I have my doubts as to whether you would happily last out the six months stipulated in the contract. You would soon miss the hustle and bustle and social activities you are used to, and the company of stimulating people of your own age."

"On the contrary, Mr. Sheil," I assured him. "One of the reasons I applied for this particular job was to get away from all that."

He shot me an inquiring look.

"You aren't going into seclusion on the rebound from an unhappy love affair, are you?" he asked anxiously.

I laughed.

"No! No! It's nothing like that!" I assured him. "I am quite fancy free, so there won't

11

even be an ardent lover rushing up to Ard-craig to distract me from my work!"

"I'm glad to hear that!" he replied, eyes flirting with me, as I had no doubt they would flirt with any attractive female. "It means I shall have no competition should I decide to come north some time! I happen to have a number of elderly clients in and around Ardcraig," he explained. "Clients like the Briartons, whom I inherited from my late father, who had a legal practice in the area.

"I make a point of visiting them all once or twice a year. This personal interest means a lot to older people, you know, so you may be seeing me again about the end of April, or the beginning of May!"

"That would be nice," I replied, delighted at the way this very attractive man did not try to hide the fact he would like to meet me again. "I take it you are definitely offering me the job, then?"

He nodded.

"Yes, Miss Gilbert. I know that you are the right person for my client."

He glanced at his watch, and frowned, as if he hadn't realised how late it was.

With an abrupt gesture he pushed his chair back still further, at the same time picking up a sealed envelope from the desk, and stood up.

"You will find your fare, and all the instructions how to get to Ardcraig and Matfield House in here," he said, handing the envelope to me.

"Unfortunately," he went on, ruefully, "I'm afraid I shall have to end our interview now. I have an appointment with one of my rather demanding elderly clients at two o'clock, which means that now I shall just have time to dictate a letter to Mrs. Briarton about the outcome of my morning interviews, and snatch a quick lunch at the club next door, before my other old lady arrives!"

I picked up my handbag from the desk.

"I'm afraid I took up rather too much of your time with all my queries, Mr. Sheil," I remarked, putting the envelope he had given me into the side pouch, then pulling on my leather, fur-lined gloves.

"I've enjoyed meeting you, Miss Gilbert," there was warmth in his tone. "I only wish we could have had more time together. I would have liked to learn more about the interesting job you are giving up, to go to Matfield."

He escorted me to the door of his private office, put his fingers on the handle, hesitated before opening the door, then turned to me with a quizzical look.

"Yes," he said frankly, "I would like to get to know you better, Miss Gilbert, and if it wasn't for Mrs. Hart," he stopped short, as if he had changed his mind about what he was going to add, and said instead, "Miss Gilbert, are you by any chance free to lunch with me to-day?"

I shot him a surprised glance as a slow surge of pleasure welled through my veins, and my pulse beats quickened with the natural re-action a woman feels when she realises that a man she finds attractive feels the same way about her.

"W-Well," I stuttered, "I had planned to return to Dundee directly after our talk, possibly taking a snack at a hotel on my way home."

"That sounds rather dull," he grimaced. "Before you start on your homeward journey, why not have lunch with me? I shall get my secretary to book a table for us at Prestonfield House," he took my acceptance for granted. "I expect you know how to get there?"

I nodded.

"Yes. I do."

"Good. Then I shall meet you there at one o'clock, on the dot!"

Smilingly he ushered me from his room

and across the hall to the reception desk.

"I am glad I can celebrate your acceptance of the job with you!"

"But Mr. Sheil!" I suddenly remembered about his other appointment. "If you have to be back here for two o'clock, it's hardly worth going out to Prestonfield!"

"Not to worry, Miss Gilbert," he assured me. "I am going to cancel that appointment. It wasn't important. More of a social visit than anything."

"Molly," he paused beside the desk to look down at his secretary. "Would you telephone Mrs. Hart please? Tell her I have been held up by important business, and I shall have to postpone our meeting."

The secretary gave him a disapproving look.

"Mrs. Hart will be disappointed. She looks forward to seeing you."

"I know, Molly," he grimaced, "but you could hardly call ours a business meeting, whereas I do still have several important matters to discuss with Miss Gilbert, now that she has decided to accept Mrs. Briarton's job," he said smoothly.

Molly directed a sullen, disbelieving, jealous glance towards me, clearly indicating that she thought I was corrupting her idol.

"Mrs. Hart will be very upset," she sniffed.

15

"Nonsense!" Sheil assured her. "You know perfectly well the old dear only comes here for a chat and a free cup of coffee, because she has nothing better to do with her time! I have to put business first!"

"But she was coming here on business to-day," persisted Molly. "She is worried about the new Income Tax rulings."

"She is always worried about something or other!" sighed Sheil. "You should know by now that worry is her hobby! However, if it will make you feel happier," he cajoled his secretary with his engaging smile, "Tell her that to make up for to-day's disappointment, I shall take her to the George for lunch tomorrow, and there we can discuss her problems in a more congenial atmosphere than the office one! That will please her, don't you think?"

"Oh, yes!" Molly's faith in her idol was restored. "She will enjoy that! I shall get in touch with her right away."

"Mr. Sheil, I hope I am not disrupting your day's programme," I murmured as he followed me to the main door.

"You are making it for me!" he replied in a low voice so that Molly, who was still watching us, would not hear. "See you at one!"

He stood in the office doorway, waiting

until the commissionaire moved forward to open the outer door of the building for me, to give me a final, friendly wave.

I shivered as I stepped from the warmth of the centrally heated office block into the chilly atmosphere of the street, and hastily turned up the fur collar of my winter coat to protect my neck from the biting cold of the keen wind which gusted round me.

I hurried to George Street, to do some shopping there, before returning to the car park where I had left my Fiat, and thence to drive quickly out to Prestonfield House to keep my one o'clock luncheon appointment.

I smiled to myself, pleased at the impression I had made on Murray Sheil, and even more pleased that I was going to enjoy his company for another hour or so on this dreary, depressing early January day.

I had liked what I had seen of the young lawyer; liked the way he had handled our interview, and admired the skilful way he had rearranged his appointments to suit himself, at the same time keeping his other client happy and mollifying his pretty secretary!

No wonder he had made a success of his profession at a comparatively early age. I judged him to be in his early thirties, and the luxurious trappings of his office, and the style of clothes he affected, told me he earned a pretty penny for himself by his astuteness!

It was a couple of minutes after one when I parked my Fiat near the entrance to the hotel, alongside a gleaming scarlet sports car.

Murray Sheil was already waiting for me in the cocktail bar, pretending not to be interested in the flirtative looks cast in his direction by a couple of young girls who were surveying his tall, lean figure, in its well cut suit, Italian silk shirt, and Gucci tie, with approving eyes.

The way he smiled at me when he saw me, and came forward to meet me, would have made most female hearts, young and old alike, flutter, as mine was doing, and I could appreciate how disappointed old Mrs. Hart would have been, if he hadn't arranged an alternative meeting with her to make up for the one he had cancelled to-day!

Over lunch, I learned a few more details about my future employer.

She had met Brigadier Briarton, of Matfield House, Ardcraig, in Cairo, towards the end of World War Two. She had been an auxiliary nurse in the field hospital where he had been a patient.

He was a childless widower. She was a widow whose only son had been killed in action at Tobruk the same year that her first husband had been drowned when the ship he commanded was torpedoed. They were both middle-aged; both lonely and in alien surroundings; both found the other attractive. They were married within weeks of their first meeting.

When the war ended, they returned to the Brigadier's family home on the outskirts of a small village in the West of Scotland, where they lived a quiet, uneventful life, enjoying their mutual hobby of gardening, and together, over the years, they turned Matfield and its gardens into a show piece.

The Brigadier had died suddenly the previous October, to his widow's surprise, for she had always thought of him as a wealthy man, leaving her only a pittance.

"What Mrs. Briarton hadn't realised," Murray told me, "and what I think her husband, in fairness, should have told her, was that he had been using his capital to keep Matfield going."

He shook his head.

"A house like that, kept in the immaculate condition in which it was kept, simply swallows money, and gives no return. I tried to tell the Brigadier each time he asked me to advise him about what shares to sell, but he would never listen, and now his wife has to bear the brunt. I don't think he realised that his pensions would not be paid after his death, and that she would be left with so little.

"Mark you, she is as stubborn about keeping Matfield in all its glory as he was, and she too refuses to listen to me when I tell her she can't afford its upkeep, and would be better off, selling the house and putting the proceeds into an investment trust.

"She says as long as she has a few pounds in the kitty, she will try to keep the place going."

"Hadn't she any income of her own, from her first husband?"

Murray shook his head.

"Not that I know of. Actually, it is rather a pity the Brigadier didn't leave her the Home Farm. She could have sold that without a qualm, and what she would have got for it would have kept Matfield flourishing until she died, unless, of course, she lived to be a centenarian, but that isn't likely, since she suffers from some sort of heart complaint."

"I thought you said the Brigadier had no family, so who got the Home Farm?" I asked, puzzled.

The young lawyer's lips tightened grimly.

"He had no direct heirs, but Tim Briarton, his great nephew, managed to wheedle his way into the old man's affections.

"As a boy and a young man, he spent a great deal of time at Matfield. His parents emigrated to New Zealand, but he went to boarding school, and later to College in this country, and he would stay with the Brigadier during part of his holidays. He always pretended a great interest in the old man's harebrained schemes as to what he would do with the Home Farm when the sitting tenants finally left and he took over, and Tim promised he would help him carry out his plans."

"Which was why he was left the place, I suppose?"

Murray shrugged.

"He was a Briarton, too, of course, but I don't see him keeping on the farm. I understand he is modernising it, to sell it at a profit. He is not so stupid when it comes to money as his great uncle, or his great aunt for that matter!

"She is even less likely to make a profit from her diaries, as he would have done carrying out the Brigadier's dream of making a profit from breeding deer to sell the venison!"

"Surely," I frowned, "knowing how badly off his great aunt now is, he will let her have some of the profit he makes from the farm?"

"That's something I must warn you not to talk about. Mrs. Briarton refuses to let anyone know her circumstances. She is a very proud woman, and would never ask for charity, although she so badly needs the money to keep Matfield as it was. That is why she has got this idea in her head that she will make money from her memoirs — which is where you come in!

"She would have tried to write her story herself, but she suffers from arthritis in her right hand, and also, as she pointed out, she wouldn't know how to set about editing her diaries, to make them readable."

"It's just possible," I said hopefully, "that her diaries will make interesting reading, and find a publisher, like the Diary of a Country Lady did. There is a vogue for that sort of thing at the moment.

"It's even possible that she has led a more exciting life than you imagine!"

"In Ardcraig?" Sheil laughed. "Hardly! If she had ever done anything exciting there, it would have been common knowledge!"

"Still," I persisted, "if she is a local personage, the area newspaper might be interested enough to print a few extracts of her life story, although what she would be paid wouldn't cover my month's salary."

I looked at him anxiously.

"Do you think she is throwing away money employing me? Perhaps you should tell her you can get no one to take the job," I began, but he interrupted me.

"That wouldn't be any good. If I didn't find someone, she is so stubborn she would try to find someone for herself, and no doubt end up with someone quite unsuitable, whereas you, Julie," he smiled across the table at me, "you fill the bill beautifully."

"Perhaps I could talk her out of the idea when I get there," I said brightly. "She might listen to me."

I was surprised to find myself so concerned for an old lady I had never seen, but whose fortitude and gallantry impressed me.

"I doubt it. Mrs. Briarton is as stubborn as they come, Julie. I have already gone over the difficulties and drawbacks of her scheme with her a dozen times, but she is quite determined to go ahead.

"As a matter of fact," he went on slowly, "I sometimes wonder if all this talk of publishing her diaries is genuine, and if she is making them an excuse to have another woman in the house; someone she can talk to and lean on a little; someone to help her over a bad patch, without her admitting to herself she can't cope; someone to relieve, if only for a few months, the terrible desolation she must be feeling following the death of her husband.

"They were never parted, even for a day, I believe, from the moment they took up residence at Matfield, and that is all of thirty-five years ago!

"You see," he nodded, "To a proud old lady like Mrs. Briarton, having a secretary would appeal more than the idea of employing an ordinary companion!"

"I still don't see how she can afford my salary, if she is as hard up as you indicate."

"She has it all worked out. She can afford you for exactly six months. She told me she looked on the outlay as a gamble which she hoped would pay off in the form of a best seller!"

He grinned at me his devilishly attractive grin.

"Do you think you can write a best seller in six months, Julie?"

"Well, if I don't produce one for Mrs. Briarton, I hope to be able to produce one of my own in that time! As I told you earlier, it was with a view to having peace and quiet and plenty of leisure to write a novel I have been thinking about for some time, that I applied for this particular job. It seemed tailor-made for me!"

"Let's talk about you now, and not my old lady," coaxed Murray. "I want to know more about you and your work. I am intrigued by both!"

During the rest of the meal we talked and talked. We talked about my past employment and my future hopes of making a living as a free lance writer. He told me about his own hope to take part again in a Monte Carlo Rally.

"I thought only works teams went in for that nowadays?" I said.

"There are always a few private entries. I did quite well last year, until the last day, when I crashed and my car was a complete write off. Next year I might be luckier!

"You know, as a boy, it was my ambition to be a racing driver — another James Clark or Jackie Stewart, but I couldn't get any backers, so in the end I had to settle down and follow in my father's footsteps and become a lawyer.

"Still," he added, "This job has its compensations!"

He smiled at me over the rim of his coffee cup.

"If I hadn't been Mrs. Briarton's lawyer, I wouldn't have met you!"

I blushed, and in an attempt to cover my confusion I said tritely, "I am sure you say that to all your women clients!"

"You aren't a client!" he pointed out, "but speaking of clients reminds me, Julie, that I would be very grateful if you would let me know how Mrs. Briarton gets along, and if she has any money or other problems I might be able to help her out with. She isn't really used to handling business matters, because she always left that kind of thing in the Brigadier's hands, so as an old friend of the family, I would like to be able to help her out if need be."

He accompanied me out to my car, pausing on the way to pluck a sprig of yellow jasmine which bloomed against the sheltered wall of the building. He tucked it into the buttonhole of my coat.

"Something to remember me by!" he smiled, holding open my car door for me.

"Good luck with your new job, Julie," he went on. "I promise I shall come to Matfield later in the year, to find out how you are getting on."

While I was fastening my seat belt, I saw him get into the smart scarlet Porsche which was parked alongside my own car.

"I wish I could afford one of those!" I called to him enviously.

"Write that best seller you've been talking about, and you will!" he chaffed, then started the engine and went speeding off down the drive ahead of me.

I soon lost sight of the Porsche in the swirling fog which was descending over the city, a fog which forced me to reduce my speed to a snail's pace as it shrouded the outlines of the grey houses with its gossamer swirls, and blurred the headlights of approaching cars, whose drivers were going as slowly as I was, for fear of skidding on the icy cobbles.

The fog even penetrated into the interior of the car, and I shivered with a sudden sensation of panic.

I hate fog. There is something repellent about it. It frightens me. Makes me feel uneasy.

Fog is something which can't be wiped away and dispersed by windscreen wipers in the way they can disperse snow and rain and frost from the glass in front of one.

Fog stays there, with you, wrapping its clammy mesh around you, imprisoning you in its folds, so that you can't escape it, as a fly is trapped in the cocoon of fine webbing which the spider wraps round it, in spite of its most desperate struggles.

I shivered again, and this time it wasn't

the pentrating cold which caused the sudden movement, but the strangest premonition of some imminent disaster, the feeling my mother used to describe as "a goose walking over one's grave."

It was a premonition which lingered with me throughout the long, slow, dreary, fogbound journey across Fife, to the Tay Bridge, and only when I drove over the bridge, into the fog free air of Angus, and saw the glittering, welcoming lights of my own home town, did the cold feeling of fear and uneasiness evaporate with the vanishing mists.

Two

It was another cold and foggy day when I left home a week later to travel to Glasgow, where I boarded a train which would take me north to the junction for Ardcraig.

Since I was to have the use of Mrs. Briarton's car as one of the "perks", of the job, I had decided that it would be stupid to drive north in my own little Fiat, since there had been reports of heavy snow falls and near "white out" conditions in parts of the Highlands. I had no desire to get stuck in a drift on some lonely stretch of roadway, where I might have to wait for hours for someone to come and rescue me.

In any case, it was pleasant not to have to concentrate on road conditions and to be able to sit back in the corner seat of an empty compartment and find time to admire the rugged scenery through which the train chugged its way.

It was so intensely cold the further north

we went that from time to time the windows iced over and I had to breathe on them to help soften the frosting, so that I could rub a spyhole on the glass with the back of my gloved hand in order once again to catch a glimpse of the countryside through which I was travelling.

By mid-afternoon the snow ceased falling, and I could now make out towering mountains, their glistening flanks and peaks reflecting the golden glow of the orange coloured sun. Snow weighed down the plumes of the pine trees which climbed the higher slopes, and gave a skeletal appearance to the bare branches of the larches on the lower reaches.

Below the embankment, pools of water had frozen to solid ice, through which needle sharp reeds and rushes protruded forlornly. In the fields, clumps of brittle dead bracken leaves and long withered ragworts, powdered with snow, stood lifeless and immobile.

The frozen scene emphasized the bleakness and loneliness of this part of the world, realistically bringing home to me how isolated I was going to be in the remote house, miles away from the equally remote village, where I was going to spend the next six months.

For the first time I had a stirring of doubt as to the wisdom of the impulse which had prompted me to give up a lively, interesting and well paid job in the home town where I had plenty of friends to call on for companionship if need be, to take on what promised to be a rather dull task of helping an octogenarian rewrite her dreary memoirs in the hope that they might find a publisher.

The one thing which had attracted me to the job had been the fact that I would not be interrupted by these friends of mine when I got down, as I hoped to do, to writing the novel I had been dreaming of for years. Now, thinking things over, surely I could have done so, merely by exerting some will power, in the comfort of my own little flat overlooking the lovely Tay estuary, rather than in an unknown house, in a cold, lonely part of the West Highlands, with an unknown employer as likely to disturb my concentration as my friends would have done?

I sighed.

There wasn't much I could do about it now. The die had been cast, and I would have to make the best of what lay ahead, with the hope that my temporary exile would prove profitable to my writing career.

The orange ball of the sun disappeared

abruptly behind a fast moving snow cloud.

With its disappearance, the scene changed. It was as if a lamp had been switched off. The golden glow vanished from the hillsides and the grey whiteness which succeeded it made the countryside appear even gloomier, as fresh flurries of flakes swirled down the gullies, becoming thicker and thicker, until the entire outside world was blotted out by the blizzard which now enveloped the train.

I huddled back into my seat, relieved when a few minutes later a voice announced over the loud speaker system, that the train would shortly be arriving at Ardcraig junction.

This was the station where according to my instructions, I was to be met by someone who would drive me the final miles to Matfield House.

I stood up stiffly, pulled my cases down from the luggage rack, and the moment the train came to a halt, I pushed open the carriage door.

A gust of bone freezing wind almost slammed it shut again, and it was with some difficulty I managed to descend on the snow thick platform, and make my way towards the ticket collector.

"Signorina Gilbert!"

I shot a startled glance over the shoulder of the uniformed railway official when I heard my name called out.

A stout little man, in a tight fitting black overcoat, with a black cossack hat perched on his head, and a pert, Hercule Poirot type moustache dusted with snow, came rushing towards me.

"Signorina!" he beamed a welcome, grabbing hold of my cases as if he had not the slightest doubt that I was the person he had come to meet, although a number of other passengers had descended from the train, and were following in my wake.

"Signorina Gilbert," he continued to smile at me. "I am glad the train was not delayed. On a day like this, you must have had such a cold journey! You will be glad to arrive, vero?"

He didn't give me time to reply before adding, "Come! This way," he continued, his soft Italian voice lilting cheerfully. "The car is over here, by the exit. But walk carefully," he warned. "There is ice beneath the snow just there," he nodded towards a rutted mound which he carefully skirted.

"I am Pino, by the way," he flashed me another brilliant smile as he dumped my cases beside a snow-covered car, and fumbled to open the door for me. "I am what Mrs. Briarton calls her right-hand man!"

He heaved my luggage into the boot, and scrambled round to the driving seat, energetically knocking the slush from his shoes before getting behind the wheel, and then rubbing his hands together to restore some warmth to his fingers, all the time admiring me with typical Italian candour.

"The Signora Briarton was pleased you were the one her lawyer selected from the list of applicants she sent him," he informed me cheerily. "She likes to have young people round her. She says it keeps her young herself! That is why she is so happy that her great nephew decided to stay on at Matfield while his own farmhouse is being modernised, and why she was delighted when my niece, Angelina, came over here a year ago, to take over the duties of housekeeper."

As I fastened my seat belt, I shot a surprised glance at the man by my side.

Murray Sheil hadn't explained to me that there were living-in members of staff at Matfield, and I had assumed that Mrs. Briarton lived alone in the house.

I was also interested to learn that Tim Briarton was also a member of the household, and I was quite sure that Murray hadn't known that the great nephew, about whom he had spoken so disparagingly, was resident at Matfield.

Possibly Mrs. Briarton had failed to mention the fact to him, since it didn't really concern him, or she may even have decided quite deliberately not to tell him, sensing, as I had done, that there was an antagonism between the two men.

Pino slipped the car into gear, and drove off. By the time we had travelled a couple of hundred yards, he was humming a pleasant old Italian ditty. I grinned to myself, wondering just how long it would be before the hum changed to an operatic aria!

Already my spirits, which had plummeted during the journey by train, were beginning to rise again. I certainly hadn't expected to find such a diverting character as Pino at Matfield, and I wondered what other surprises would be in store for me when I reached the old house.

The snow had eased off when we left the station yard, and as the sky swiftly cleared, the setting sun radiated an amber glow over mountain and meadow and across the waters of the sea loch which flanked the road, until we turned right, away from it, into a narrower road, bordered by spinneys of graceful silver birches, whose leafless branches cast an intricate pattern of shadows across the snow.

The car tyres crunched noisily over the frozen ruts, almost drowning out Pino's pleasant singing voice, as we drove on, for several miles, before turning right again, into an even narrower lane, which led across low lying fields, with the storm flecked waters of the loch visible once again, this time on either side of us.

Soon we came to a high wall, with an arched gateway, leading into a curving drive bordered by very tall, evergreen rhododendrons, whose leaves sagged under the weight of snow.

Seconds after turning into the driveway, I had my first view of Matfield House, a two storeyed manor house, with a central, pillared portico, and on either side of the rectangular façade, turretted wings, which seemed to be of a later date than the original building.

The westering sun was low in the sky behind us, and its light, more scarlet now than orange, striking against the mullioned windows, reflected back from the panes on to the snow in the garden below, giving the effect of splashes of blood across a white sheet.

For no good reason, the feeling of euphoria I had experienced since my meeting with the friendly little Italian houseman vanished.

For a moment the strange premonition I had had a week earlier, when I left Prestonfield House to follow Murray back to Edinburgh, returned. It was as if some primitive instinct was warning me that some danger threatened me. I controlled a shiver of fear with difficulty.

"Here we are!" Pino stopped singing and turned to me with a grin on his wrinkled face. "Matfield House! It is beautiful, is it not?" he sighed with admiration.

I wasn't sure if the admiration was for his mistress's lovely house, or for me, for he kept on looking at me approvingly!

Pino's admiration, his infectious grin, immediately chased away my fearful forebodings and made me laugh at myself for my moment of near panic.

I was in less danger in this quiet, picturesque place than I would have been in any city, where at times even trying to cross a street can be a hazard!

I unfastened my seat belt. Pino opened the car door for me, and gallantly helped me out, in case I should slip when I put my feet on the frozen ground.

While he went to the boot to get my cases, I walked slowly towards the portico.

The shallow steps leading to the doorway

had been swept clear of snow, although it still lay inches thick on the curving stone balustrade which flanked them, and on the enormous, Grecian styled stone flower urns which stood on either side of the thick wooden front door.

I stretched out my hand to pull the bell chain, but before I could do so the door was opened wide by a slim, dark-haired, and very lovely young woman.

"This is my niece Angelina, Signorina Gilbert," announced Pino as he came up behind me with my luggage.

Angelina murmured a polite greeting, then ushered me through a stone flagged vestibule into a large, octagonal hall which, in spite of its size and its high ceiling, which extended to a central glass dome on the roof, was surprisingly cosy, although no doubt any interior would have seemed warm after the freezing cold outside.

"I shall take you to your suite of rooms right away, Signorina Gilbert," Angelina announced briskly, leading the way towards the staircase while Pino followed us with my cases.

"I am sure you will wish to freshen yourself up after your long journey, before you meet Signora Briarton."

I was surprised at her command of English, which she spoke even better than her uncle, and would have remarked on it, if she hadn't gone hurrying ahead of me at such a pace, into a carpeted corridor to the left of the main stairway, to open a pine door at the far end, which revealed another, narrower staircase, which led to the turret wing I was to occupy during my stay at Matfield.

I was thrilled when my new quarters were shown to me, for here was a complete flat, with a small bedroom, living room, bathroom and minute kitchenette — the kind of flatlet whose rent would have taken a considerable chunk out of my salary in any city, and a flatlet, moreover, which would give me quiet and privacy to devote my leisure hours to my novel.

Angelina hovered in the background while Pino deposited my cases in the bedroom, and explained to me that in case of fire, there was a fire escape on the other side of the door at the top of the stairs, which led into the main part of the building, and that this door must never be locked.

When her uncle left us, Angelina told me briskly that Mrs. Briarton would receive me in the living room, which was the room on the ground floor to the right of the front door.

"Don't take too long to tidy yourself," she went on, her brown eyes fixed on me; brown eyes which assessed me much as her uncle's had done, but which showed neither his admiration nor his friendliness.

"I shall be serving afternoon tea in ten minutes, and Mrs. Briarton does not like to be kept waiting for her meals."

She left the room quietly, and I looked after her, puzzled by her attitude. Angelina was not at all pleased that I had come here. I wondered why. In her place, living in such an isolated spot, I would have been pleased to have the company of another woman of my own age.

Perhaps she felt that I might regard her as an inferior, since she was the housekeeper, and I was the private secretary. Perhaps she was reserved by nature. What did it matter anyway?

I washed my face and hands, brushed my shoulder length hair, whose colour, in the soft glow of the dressing table light, reminded me of the sunlit fronds of the bracken I had seen earlier in the fields by the embankment.

My hand trembled with a quiver of trepidation at the thought of coming face to face in a few minutes with my new employer, and the movement smudged the eye shadow

I was applying to the lids above my blue-grey eyes.

I scolded myself for being so silly as I finished applying my make-up, straightened the skirt of my gold woollen two piece suit, and re-tied the brown and gold spotted silk square round my slender throat.

It was idiotic to feel nervous like this! I was twenty-five. I had held down a skilled and demanding job to my recent employer's satisfaction for four years. I had an excellent academic record. I usually got on well with people, so why should I get up tight about meeting an eighty year old woman, autocratic though I gathered she was both from Murray Sheil's description of her, and from Angelina's warning that Mrs. Briarton did not like to be kept waiting.

Indeed, it was more than likely that the old lady was as nervous at meeting someone like me as I was feeling at this moment!

Pino was hovering in the main hall, to greet me when he saw me emerge from the side corridor with almost the identical words Angelina had spoken.

"The Signora Briarton is waiting for you in the living room. I am glad you did not take long to freshen up. She does not like to be kept waiting, especially," he added, a note of affection creeping into his voice,

41

"when she is so excited about meeting you! This is quite an event for her!"

He bustled ahead of me across the hall, and opened a door set flush with the polished wooden panelling of the wall.

"Signora Briarton, this is Signorina Gilbert," he announced somewhat pompously, ushering me into a square, spacious room, where the dancing gold flames from a crackling log fire were reflected on the highly polished pine-wood floor, the highly polished furniture, and the overhead, central chandelier, whose dripping crystal tears shivered into tinkling music with the draught from the still open door.

"Thank you, Pino. That will be all!"

The slim, erect woman, who was standing with her back to the window, the last dying embers of the stormy sunset making a golden halo of her white, softly waved hair, dismissed the man in a pleasant voice.

She waited until the door closed behind him before moving stiffly forward in my direction, to address me.

"So you are the young woman Murray decided I would be able to get on with?"

Shrewd blue eyes studied me with interest, noting every detail of my appearance, from my smoothly brushed hair to the gleaming toes of the high heeled shoes which had replaced the damp snow boots I had travelled in.

"I expect, if he is as shrewd in his assessment of character as his father was, he has made the right choice!" She smiled at me.

"On the other hand," the old eyes flashed mischievously, "he could have been hoodwinked by a very pretty girl, but I doubt it. Murray is used to pretty girls. He usually has one on tow. He is also a very smart young lawyer, and smart young lawyers shouldn't allow themselves to be hoodwinked, should they?"

I hoped the firelight disguised the flush which crept into my cheeks at her teasing words.

"Mr. Sheil decided I had the right qualifications, and after a long conversation, the right personality for the job, Mrs. Briarton. He was quite sure we would get on together."

The old lady continued to regard me steadily, and under her gaze I was conscious of a renewed nervousness. Somehow, I had thought that I would be dealing with an unworldly old lady, who would be impressed by my sophistication and my qualifications, but Mrs. Briarton was not in the least what I had imagined she would be like. She was far from the twittery, unsophisticated, cossetted country woman, interested only in her home and garden, I had pictured her to be.

There was an aura about her, of strength of character and intelligence and, thank goodness, of humour which gave me a hopeful inkling, which I hadn't been given from Murray's description of her, that helping her with her memoirs might not be quite such a dull job as I had anticipated!

"Do sit down, my dear," she invited, lowering herself slowly into the firmly upholstered settee facing the fire, and patting the seat beside her to show me where she wanted me to sit.

As I did as I was bidden, she turned her head towards the door.

"Ah! I can hear Angelina coming with the tea trolley!"

She turned back to me.

"I am sure you will be glad of a refreshing cup after your long and trying journey. I know I always was when I had been travelling for hours!"

While the housekeeper trundled the trolley through the door towards us, I studied Mrs. Briarton's averted face, which was fully illumined with the glow from the fire and the softer light of the table lamp.

A myriad wrinkles crinkled the skin round

her mouth, her nose, her eyes, but her cheeks were still smooth and soft and pink, almost unnaturally youthful for the eighty years she had lived.

Her hands, however, certainly betrayed her age. Brown spots showed up on the creased skin, and the fingers, gnarled and twisted with arthritis, were the hands of an old woman.

I noticed, too, that she had difficulty in holding the lorgnette which she now raised to her eyes, to study my own features more carefully from close range.

While Angelina set out the cups on the long coffee table in front of us, and poured the tea from a fine Wedgwood pot, Mrs. Briarton's gaze came to rest on my own slim hands, which were still faintly tanned from the Alpine sun I had enjoyed during my Christmas holiday spent on the ski slopes near Grenoble.

"I see you are still fancy free," she indicated my ringless engagement finger with her lorgnette.

"You are wise, my dear, very wise, not to rush into a hasty, youthful marriage.

"I did, you know," she shook her head. "But it wasn't a success. No! It wasn't a success," she repeated sadly.

"I was too young. Too selfish. I wanted to

45

take, take, take all the time. Never to give. Everything had to be my way! It was this selfishness, my youthful ignorance, my waywardness, yes, and my wilfulness, which led me into a strange, unnatural world all those long years ago!

"I think," she shook her head, "you are in for a surprise when you read my early life story, my dear. I don't think," her blue eyes twinkled, "my memoirs will make such dull reading as you may have been imagining they would!"

A tingle of anticipation feathered down my spine.

Was it possible that the diaries I had come to Matfield to edit weren't going to be so deadly boring and non eventful as I had imagined; as Murray Sheil had led me to believe they would be?

For the first time, I felt a thrill of excitement at the prospect of the work I had undertaken to do.

However, I would not have felt so happily excited about my future task, if I had guessed just how deadly, in a literal way, these diaries would turn out to be!

THREE

I hadn't been the only one who had been listening, held in thrall by what Mrs. Briarton was saying.

Angelina, who had been standing beside the tea trolley, ready to pour out the tea, was staring at her employer, eyes agog with curiosity, as eager to learn more of the old lady's past as I was.

A log in the fire crackled suddenly with a sharp fusillade of sound, making me jump, making Angelina start as well, so that she knocked the spout of the teapot noisily against the rim of the cup into which she had been pouring the tea.

Her movement reminded Mrs. Briarton that we were not alone, and she turned to the housekeeper with a frown.

"Angelina, I thought you had gone," she said in a tone of vexation. "Now that Miss Gilbert is staying with me, she will do the pouring in future."

"Very well, Signora," Angelina replied, at the same time bending down to place the teapot on the trivet in the hearth, by this gesture hiding from Mrs. Briarton the flash of annoyance which crossed her face.

She straightened up slowly and, her face once more expressionless, asked, "Is there anything else you wish me to do for you now, Signora?"

"Why, yes!" Mrs. Briarton nodded. "If you happen to see young Mr. Briarton, would you tell him I would like him to join us here for afternoon tea?

"I haven't seen him to-day, because he left the house before I was up, and there was something I wanted to ask him."

For the first time since I had met her, Angelina's slightly disdainful manner deserted her.

"I shall go and look for him at once," she said eagerly, glancing up at her reflection in the oval, gold-framed mirror which hung over the mantelpiece, smoothing her hair from her forehead, and tightening the leather belt which encircled her neat waist.

I tried not to smile.

It seemed that the lovely Angelina had a soft spot for Mrs. Briarton's great nephew. I wondered what he was like, to catch this pretty girl's interest. Was he good looking?

Was he as attractive as Murray? Or was it that he was the only male of about Angelina's own age in the neighbourhood?

The housekeeper hurried from the room and I glanced hopefully at Mrs. Briarton, expecting her to return to the subject of her life story now that Angelina had departed.

Instead, she switched to quite a different topic, talking of Pino and Angelina, since I had earlier expressed an interest in them.

"I am so lucky to have the pair of them with me here," she said. "Without them, I don't know what I should do. It is quite impossible to get help in this part of the world, unless someone casually, for an odd hour or so, which is no good as far as I am concerned.

"Pino is such a dear man!" she sighed. "You can have no idea how kind and understanding he was when Charles was so ill, and how he comforted me when he died. I really don't know how I could have carried on, without his discreet and constant help."

Tears brightened her blue eyes.

"Yes, after my Brigadier died, if it hadn't been for Pino, and, of course, Tim, I would have been quite lost. They were the props which helped sustain me," she sniffed, dabbing at her eyes with a wisp of white cotton.

"I got rather a surprise when Pino met

me at the station," I said, tactfully steering the subject from her husband's death. "The last person I expected to have as my escort here was a delightful Italian who entertained me with a repertoire of Neapolitan love songs as we drove from the station!"

Mrs. Briarton blinked back her tears, giving me a watery smile of approval for my effort to cheer her.

"Yes. Pino is a long way from his native Napoli here, but he has always remained a Neapolitan at heart, even although he hasn't been back to his homeland for almost twenty years!

"Do you know," she went on to explain, "Pino has lived in Ardcraig even longer than I have!

"He came to this part of the world as a prisoner-of-war after his capture in the North African Campaign and was given work on the Matfield estate.

"He liked it so much here, because conditions were so much better than in his native land at that time, he decided to stay on after the war was over, and sent for his wife Maria to join him.

"She acted as housekeeper here until she died over a year ago. After some months Pino suggested that his niece Angelina, who lived in Cortina, but who had a notion to work in this country, might be interested in taking her aunt's place.

"I wasn't very sure about it, since she was so young, and so pretty," went on Mrs. Briarton, "but she has fitted in very well, and seems to be happy enough, especially now that one of her compatriots has come over to work as a ski instructor in the new Ski Centre in Ardcraig.

"I only hope he won't take her back to Italy with him!" she sighed. "It would be impossible to replace her, for I certainly could not afford to pay the wages I understand other housekeepers are demanding nowadays."

She moved restlessly in her chair.

"This place costs so much to maintain, even with the minimum of help, Miss Gilbert. I think, if I had had the remotest idea what it took to run Matfield, and certainly, if I had had the remotest idea that Charles was leaving me so little, I would never have promised him, on his deathbed, that I would keep it on, and in the way he would like it to be kept.

"Indeed," she sighed, "I don't think Charles realised just how little money there was left in his trust fund, or he would never have extracted the promise from me.

"However, a promise is a promise, and I

51

am not going to let Charles down, although you can imagine how it has been worrying me, thinking up ways and means of finding cash!"

A sharp sneeze from other side of the door made Mrs. Briarton turn round sharply.

She shook her head and smiled ruefully.

"In spite of her eagerness to seek Tim out, I'm afraid that Angelina's curiosity to know if we would be discussing my past life once again after she had left the room, got the better of her!

"She is a delightful young woman, and I am very fond of her, but she has three weaknesses. She is vain. She has a weakness for the opposite sex, and she is very, very inquisitive!

"Listening at keyholes, reading any letters or documents which are left lying about are second nature to her, and she doesn't seem to see anything wrong in such activities.

"I am telling you this so that you will be careful what you say in her hearing, if you don't want your secrets broadcast, for she moves so quietly you sometimes don't realise she is quite near by.

"And talking of secrets, Miss Gilbert, reminds me. There is one other clause I have added to your work contract; one which I did not wish to discuss with Murray, because he would have laughed at it, and said I was over estimating the importance of my diaries, and if I had insisted it was necessary, it would have roused his curiosity, and I didn't want to do that, in case he tried to wheedle my secrets from me."

She paused and raised her lorgnette to eye me directly.

"Miss Gilbert, this is the clause I have added. Before I give you my diaries to edit, I want you to promise me that until the work we are going to do on them is complete, and they are ready to be sent for publication, you will not reveal to a single soul the secrets you will learn from my journals!"

I gaped at her, thinking, as she said Murray would have done, that she must surely be over estimating her importance.

"I mean what I say," she returned my gaze. "The truth is, if my hands weren't so crippled. I would have preferred to write my autobiography myself, but as it is," she shrugged, "I can't do so. This is why I was so particular not only about the qualifications of the secretary I would employ, but about her character and personality. I needed someone discreet and trustworthy, and Murray had this in mind when he interviewed the people whose names I sent him, although he thought the need for discretion was because I did not want my straightened circumstances to be discussed."

"Of course I promise not to discuss your private affairs, Mrs. Briarton!" I told her, although I was of the opinion she was making a deal of fuss about matters which had taken place so long that they would be of little interest to the present generation.

She disconcerted me by reading my thoughts.

"I daresay Murray told you I was just a simple old woman who had lived a quiet, conventional country life here in Ardcraig, and that the most exciting moment he could recall of my past was when I accidentally pushed the Brigadier into Ardcraig harbour when I was asked to launch a boat for the local yacht club!"

She smiled at the reminiscence.

"Yes, I admit I have lived a somewhat quiet existence since I married Charles and came to live at Matfield, but it is not about my life at Matfield I intend to write!

"Indeed, like a great many people, Murray is going to find out that I am not quite the kind of person he imagines me to be.

"Even my dear Brigadier knew nothing about the life I led before I met and married him, and I never wanted him to find out the truth about me!

"All he knew was that I was a widow, who had joined the nursing auxiliary service after my only son and my first husband had been killed in action; that I had no other relatives, and that I was born in London, where I had lived most of my life before going to serve in Cairo.

"He was never curious about my past. He accepted me for what he thought I was — an attractive, intelligent woman, from his kind of background.

"Fortunately my name, Elizabeth Thomis meant nothing to him, but then," she shrugged, "the only pages in a newspaper which interested him were the sporting ones or the gardening column. I doubt if he had ever read a scandal sheet or a gossip column in his life, most of which was spent in India, where he made a small fortune, which would enable him to maintain the beautiful estate he would inherit one day.

"In me he saw the perfect hostess to grace the house he loved. I did not disillusion him. To me he was a man who made my life worthwhile again, and I vowed to myself never to let him down. I had buried my past, and I had no intention of exhuming it for him. He was so proud of me, so happy because I loved his home."

She uttered a sad little laugh.

"I often used to tease him that he loved Matfield House more than he loved me!"

Once again she moved restlessly in her chair, lowered her lorgnette so that she could raise her cup of tea to her lips, and sat staring into the glowing fire for several seconds before resuming her story.

"When you read my early diaries, Miss Gilbert, you will understand why I wanted to keep my past a secret from my dear Brigadier. I would never have wanted Charles to find out what sort of woman I had been!"

I wrinkled my brow in a frown as I listened to her. The name Elizabeth Thomis, or rather Lady Elizabeth Thomis, rang a faint bell in my head. It had been mentioned in a book of the Twenties which I had read not so very long ago, and it had been connected with some kind of scandal, though for the moment I could not remember the details.

A log sparked and crackled fiercely as it collapsed in two pieces onto the glowing embers on the grate below, its fiery explosion drowning out the other softer, stealthier creakings in the room, and startling me into ejaculating the words which rose to my lips, but which tact should have restrained.

"Then why do you want to resurrect that past now, Mrs. Briarton?" I exclaimed. "What good can it do to you? To anyone?"

She drew a long shuddering breath.

"What I was, my early life, can no longer hurt or dismay my beloved Brigadier, but it will help me fulfil the promise I made to him!

"Once in my life, Miss Gilbert, I broke a vow to a man I loved. The vow to love, honour and obey my first husband. I am not going to break a second sacred promise, my dear, that promise I made Charles, on his death bed, that I would maintain this beloved house as he would have maintained it, as long as I lived!

"Publishing my early life story is the only way I can see of making enough money to do this.

"No, don't interrupt, Miss Gilbert," she held up her hand to signal me to silence as I was about to speak.

"I have thought it out very carefully. I was almost at my wits' end, though, before the inspiration came, and who would have thought that it would be that absurd Margaret who would give me the idea!" she laughed shakily.

"There I was, lying in bed, reading her silly memoirs to help me fall asleep, when the thought struck me.

"If Margaret could get her life story published, and be paid well for it, as I found out, so could I! If her dull book could get into the top twenty of best sellers, mine should top the list!

"Do you know!" she suddenly gave me an infectious chuckle. "Now that I've made up my mind to go ahead with the project, I'm getting quite enthusiastic about it, especially now that I have met you, for I am sure you are the ideal person to ghost my life story for me, and we will outsell Margaret!" she chuckled again. "I'd love to see her face when she learns about me!"

She stopped talking to take another sip of tea, and I turned away from her and gazed into the fire. I felt deeply sorry for her, and I did not want her to see the pity in my eyes.

Mrs. Briarton had no idea how difficult it was to get any kind of book published, and what publisher would handle a book of memoirs by someone who was unknown? Old scandals were not of interest unless you were someone of importance, and the general public was more interested in reading about the goings on of pop stars, or T.V. personalities, or football heroes, rather than of the misty past of someone they had never heard about.

"Would you like some more tea, Mrs. Briarton?" I asked, to break the prolonged, awkward silence which had followed her chatter.

She raised her lorgnette to look at me again. There was an amused expression on her face.

"You don't think any publisher would look twice at the life story of someone like me, do you, my dear?" she demanded with disconcerting frankness.

I replied equally frankly.

"Mrs. Briarton, it is very difficult to find a publisher these days, especially for your kind of book, unless you are a very well known personality. Indeed, there is not a great deal of money to be made from writing, unless you can give the public something interesting, or novel, or, in the case of memoirs, some titillating scandals!"

"My dear Julie," she raised her white eyebrows, "I do have something interesting to write about. As for scandal, well there is nothing, as you have remarked, like the whisper of scandal in high places, scandal among the rich and famous, or infamous, to whet the public appetite, and some of the secrets my memoirs will reveal, will do just that!

"As Elizabeth Briarton, widow of Brigadier Charles Briarton, my diaries contain exactly the kind of villagey gossip I expect Murray told you to expect of me, but it is not the autobiography of Elizabeth Briarton I am asking you to help me with!

"You are going to edit my diaries from 1920 to 1943, when I was Elizabeth Thomis — Lady Elizabeth Thomis.

"You are too young, perhaps, for that name to mean anything, but it will still mean a lot to a great many people, for I was one of the most famous, or I should say, notorious, socialites of that era. My name featured in every scandal sheet, until the day I was presumed killed in a German air raid over London in 1943, when my house in Belgravia was rased to the ground.

"When you resurrect me, believe me, there is not a single editor who would reject my life story, as you will find out when you read my diaries, learn of the scandals —"

"What scandals are you discussing now, Liz?"

Mrs. Briarton turned round with a start, to look towards the doorway.

I too looked round at the unexpected interruption to see a youngish, stockily built man, with a lock of caramel coloured hair flopping untidily over his brow, come strolling across the room towards us.

FOUR

"Really, Tim!" Mrs. Briarton snapped angrily at the newcomer. "You should knock before coming into my room! I was having a private talk with Miss Gilbert!"

The man seemed taken aback by her tone.

"I am sorry, Liz," he apologised, "but Angelina came to tell me that you wanted me to join you for afternoon tea, so I took it you were expecting me, and that there was no need to stand on ceremony!"

While he was speaking, his glance strayed in my direction.

Mrs. Briarton, her cheeks still flushed with concern in case he had overheard part of our conversation, made an effort to pull herself together.

"Yes! Yes! I did send Angelina to fetch you, Tim," she replied in a flustered voice, "but I did not expect she would find you so quickly."

She turned to me.

61

"Miss Gilbert, this is Timothy Briarton, my husband's great nephew, who is staying with me here at Matfield, while his farm-house, which is quite near here, is being modernised.

"Tim, this is Julie Gilbert, my new secretary."

Briarton strode forward to take my hand in a firm grip.

"So you are the person there has been so much talk about!" he smiled at me. "We have all been wondering why Liz wants a secretary. Morag and I both offered to do any work she might need doing, but Liz would have none of it. She said she was going to surprise us all by writing a book, and our typing would not be up to that!"

Mrs. Briarton did not respond to his light-hearted raillery. She regarded him with suspicious eyes for a few seconds before demanding abruptly, "Tim, did you overhear any of our conversation when you came into the room just now?"

He shot her a surprised look.

"Merely the word 'scandal' as I opened the door," he answered with a shake of his head.

"Naturally," he added, with a glimmer of amusement in his intensely blue eyes. "I pricked up my ears!"

"Then you can unprick them!" she replied briskly. "Our discussion was not about anything which would interest you!"

"You do love your little secrets, don't you, Liz?" he laughed at her as he took the cup of tea I handed to him, but the laughter was kindly.

"What with your study whose threshold no one is allowed to cross, and these hush hush memoirs of yours you tell us you are going to write, you make us all intensely curious!"

"My dear Tim, surely you know that all women love having secrets, important or otherwise!" she smiled across at him, looking much more relaxed now that she knew he had overheard nothing of importance. "That is why the Greek Sphinx was depicted as a woman!"

"Ah! Yes!" Tim winked at me over his cup, "but a man discovered her secret in the long run, didn't he?"

"Yes, and that is what destroyed her," I said slowly, and gave an unexpected shiver.

Mrs. Briarton nodded.

"Yes. Certain secrets, when revealed, can be destructive, so don't you go prying into mine, young man!" she warned Tim. "It will do you no good to do so!"

"Now, tell me," she went on in a lighter tone. "How is the work on the farmhouse progressing? Is this weather holding things up?"

"The outside work has come to a stand-still, so I have turned my attention to what has to be done indoors. Fortunately the new bathroom units arrived before the snow-storm, so they can be fitted in."

I sat back and enjoyed my cup of tea while I listened to Mrs. Briarton and Tim talk of the alterations and improvements he was making to the old farmhouse he had inherited.

It was very pleasant to be able to sit back and relax, enjoying the warmth of the fire glow on my face, the soft comfort of the easy chair after the hardness of the seat in which I had sat so long in the train coming north.

I was almost, but not quite totally, wooed to catnapping by the pleasant surroundings, the murmur of soft voices and the pleasing tinkle of the chandelier pendants which moved with the slightest draught, but I forced myself to stay awake by watching Tim Briarton.

He was good looking, in a rather rugged way, and I liked the way the corners of his eyes crinkled when he smiled. I could understand Angelina's interest in him. I could even understand her attitude to me, now, for she might fear that I would distract his attentions from her, and from what Mrs. Briarton had said, Angelina liked the attention of young men!

I had been paying scant interest to the conversation, but now the sharpness of Mrs. Briarton's voice as she remonstrated with her great nephew alerted my notice.

"Tim!" I heard Mrs. Briarton say with a note of dismay in her voice. "You are surely not going out again tonight! It is snowing heavily again. There could be drifting with the high wind on the road between here and Ardcraig, and you could get stuck for hours!"

"I have to go out, Liz," replied Tim. "Today is Morag's birthday. She is giving a party for her guests at the Centre, and I promised to help with the drinks, since her brother is away at the moment."

"Surely there are plenty of other young men there only to eager to help her out!" sniffed Mrs. Briarton. "How about that new ski instructor, Angelina's friend?"

"I promised I would help," said Tim firmly. "In any case, I don't want to miss the party. Morag's get-togethers are always amusing."

"If you must go, you must, I suppose," Mrs. Briarton didn't seem too pleased, "but I was hoping that you would be with us at Matfield this evening, since it is Miss Gilbert's first night with us. You see the Harveys often enough."

"Morag didn't arrange for her birthday to happen to-day to annoy you, Liz!" retorted Tim flippantly. "In any case, I am sure you and Miss Gilbert will have plenty to discuss, especially those secrets of yours," he grinned, "so I would really be de trop!"

He smiled across at me, and I found myself instinctively responding to his smile.

It would have been rather pleasant to have Tim's presence this evening, I thought. He was an easy person to get on with. He had a boyish charm of manner I found appealing, and I liked his mischievous humour. I experienced an odd twinge of disappointment because he wouldn't be spending the evening with us.

Mrs. Briarton rose slowly to her feet and went over to the window. Snow was blustering against the house, great white stars of the stuff clung to the panes and obscured the view.

"I still think you are very unwise to go out tonight, Tim," she repeated obstinately. "I am sure Morag won't be expecting you now that the weather has taken a turn for the worse."

"Dear Liz, don't worry about me! I've been out in worse storms than this, and even if the car gets stuck, I could walk to the Centre. In any case," he concluded firmly, as if this put an end to the matter, "I promised Morag I would come, and a promise is a promise."

"You might get lost if you tried to walk," Liz made one final attempt to dissuade.

"Rubbish! I know the way between here and the Sports Complex so well, I could get there and back blindfolded!"

"I expect you could!" she responded tartly. "You visit the place often enough!"

"Oh, by the way," she came back to sit down on the settee and looked up at him as she was speaking. "You can tell Morag what I have already told her in my letter, although I know she thinks I shall weaken in my resolve, that I have no intention of selling any part of Matfield for her expansion plans, and particularly not the area round the loch. If she wants to acquire my land for her ambitious schemes, she can wait until I am dead, when you —" she stopped abruptly.

"Never mind, what happens then will not concern me, and I don't want to get upset thinking what my heirs may do to the place!

"Now, let's talk of something else. I am sure Miss Gilbert must be tired of listening to family gossip!"

"Poor Miss Gilbert looks as if she is having difficulty keeping her eyes open!" Briarton smiled across at me. "Don't worry about that," he twinkled, "our west coast air always seems to have this effect on visitors!"

We chatted about general subjects for a time, then Tim excused himself, and Mrs. Briarton suggested that I might like to go up to my room to unpack, while Angelina came in to clear away the afternoon tea dishes, and receive her instructions for the dinner menu that evening.

"We dine early at Matfield," Mrs. Briarton informed me as I rose to my feet. "Usually about seven thirty. I like to retire before nine o'clock."

That evening, I decided to follow my employer's example and go to bed early.

I was tired, yet at the same time too restless to sit and read or watch television, and after we had finished our post dinner coffee and the very pleasant liqueur which Pino had recommended to me, I accompanied Mrs. Briarton to the foot of the stairway, before making for the corridor which led to my own suite of rooms.

"Julie!" she called after me before I had taken a half dozen steps away from her after bidding her goodnight. "I forgot! I meant to show you the room where you will be working tomorrow. You might want to check that I have put out everything you will require."

She signed me to follow her across the hall, to the wing on the far side, along a corridor to a small, attractive chamber, lined with shelves of books on gardening, architecture, art and antiques as well as other practical subjects.

I noticed there were very few fiction books, save for leather bound editions of Dickens and Thackeray and Scott, but there were a great many books on travel, and numerous biographies and autobiographies.

"The diaries are kept under lock and key in this desk here," she indicated an elegant piece of rosewood furniture, which looked ornamental rather than practical, "but I thought you might like more work space, so Tim carried in that table for me," she nodded towards a modern teak table on which I noticed a brand new electric typewriter, boxes of typing paper, and every aid I could possibly need for the task I was to undertake.

"You will also find photographs, newspaper cuttings and scrap books for the period with which you will be concerned in the top drawer, which is also locked.

"Tomorrow morning, your first task will be to read through the 1920–1943 diaries, unless," her eyes glinted hopefully, "you don't mind working out of office hours for once, and would like to take a quick glance through them tonight, so that you would have an idea of what you are letting yourself in for!

"But no!" she decided before I could reply. "On second thoughts, that would not be a good idea. They might make indigestible night-time fare, and in any case," she eyed me frankly, "I think I would like you to have a good opinion of me for a few more hours!"

At my amused expression, she shook her head.

"I mean that, Julie!"

I was glad that she felt the ice had been sufficiently broken between us to address me informally by my Christian name.

"Now that the time has come for someone else to read my life story," she continued, "I feel decidedly odd! Like a drowning man must feel when, as they say, he sees the life he has lived flash past his eyes in the final moments."

She paused and drew a long, slow breath,

before ending in a rather quavery voice.

"My dear, I wonder what you will think of me after you read these diaries with all the secret thoughts I committed to paper in these far off days?

"Perhaps you won't even want to live under the same roof as me when you learn what I was like then!"

I eyed her askance, trying to veil my private amusement.

Poor old lady! She apparently thought of herself as having been some dreadful femme fatale with a shady and shocking past, without realising that what would have shocked her generation would be dismissed as nothing even to blink at in the present age!

At the same time, her innuendoes intrigued me. It might be quite interesting and amusing to pass an hour before going up to bed, glancing through the famous diaries!

"You have roused my curiosity to a pitch, Mrs. Briarton!" I smiled at her. "I can hardly wait until morning comes to start my first task for you. In fact, I wouldn't mind having a look through your diaries before I go to bed!"

My employer raised her lorgnette to study my face intently. After a long scrutiny, she lowered the glass, let it fall the length of the gold chain which secured it round her neck, and shrugged.

"It is up to you when you read them, Julie. Tonight. Tomorrow. What does it matter. Perhaps the sooner the better!"

She opened her handbag, awkwardly unhooked a small piece of metal from the key ring she took out, and handed it to me.

"This is the key to the desk. This is the first time it will have left my possession, so there is one thing I must ask you."

"Yes?"

"Never let it leave your possession from now on, and always make doubly sure, when you leave the study, that all documents and diaries are locked away out of sight. I want no prying eyes to see them, or to learn what is in them, until the final version of my story is ready to send out to a publisher!

"Goodnight, Julie. I hope you will sleep well after what you read. I shall see you in the breakfast room at eight-thirty."

She turned and left me standing in the study, holding the little key between my fingers, feeling strangely uneasy, as well as curious, about the secrets I was soon to uncover, and my hand seemed all thumbs as I pushed the key into the lock of the desk, turned it, removed the box marked 1920–

1943 which held a number of long, slim books, and sat down to read.

I was still reading when the grandfather clock in the corridor outside chimed four o'clock.

My eyes were sore, my head ached, my bones ached with fatigue, but still I read on, fascinated by the twenty-three neatly and vividly recorded years of a woman who had been a famous beauty of the post First World War era; a woman who had loved passionately and quarrelled equally passionately with the man she had married at eighteen; the man who, when their child was only two, wanted her to leave London, and the bright social world where she was an acknowledged star, to live with him at the back of beyond, in a tiny township in South America, where he had been appointed chief engineer on dam construction work.

She refused point blank to go. He could get a job in London, she declared imperiously. Her world was here. She wasn't going to leave it.

Her husband had been equally adamant. He had just landed the kind of work he was hankering for; something he considered worth while. He was tired of the phoney London Society in which they moved. He wanted away from it, and what was more,

73

she would have to come with him, for a wife's place was at her husband's side, and if she truly loved him, she would follow him wherever he went.

He booked their passage to Rio, thinking, right up to the last minute, she would give in and accompany him, but she didn't, so he went off, taking their son wih him, in spite of her pleas, hoping, as she then saw it, to force her hand, so that she would eventually go out and join them.

Elizabeth had been furious at not getting her own way. She determined not to join him. He would give in first, and come back home. To ensure this, to make him jealous, she indulged in a series of flirtations with friends of his, knowing news of them would reach his ears.

He wrote back, telling her not to act like a little idiot, but to grow up, and behave like a mature and responsible person, and honour her marriage vows.

She wouldn't give in. In a vain attempt to bring him home again, she told him that if he didn't return, their marriage was at an end.

When this threat met with no success, like the spoilt child she had always been, she determined to show him she meant what she said, and that she no longer cared for him, and was going to go her own way.

The series of scandalous love affairs in which she now indulged were more to provide a sop to her pride than anything else. She wanted to feel that other men found her desirable and would do anything for her, even if her husband was fool enough not to appreciate her. They also, as she confided to her diary, helped her stop thinking about the man she still loved, but whom pride prevented her from returning to.

Lady Elizabeth Thomis, as she had been then, became notorious as the wildest, least inhibited star of the gay Charleston era.

She was beautiful, amusing, and until the slump of the thirties, she had money enough of her own to indulge her whims. She was the friend, and more than friend of Royalty, of Cabinet Ministers, and of foreign diplomats, and figured in one sensational divorce case.

She danced and loved the nights away in the Café Society of London and Paris, Rome and the Riviera, and during some of these casual affairs she learned many secrets; secrets which would have startled the world, about the people with whom she associated; people who later became world famous and important, presenting a façade of respectability to the public, who admired their outward image, an image which Elizabeth could have smashed, had she chosen to do so.

Yes, there were still people alive at this date, who would sleep uneasily, if they could sleep at all, when they learned that Lady Elizabeth Thomis whom no doubt they had happily supposed dead, buried with their indiscreet past in the wreckage of her bomb-blasted house in London in 1943, was not only still alive, but about to write her memoirs and expose their true characters to the world!

I grew more and more troubled as I read on and on. Young though I was, even I knew some of the people mentioned. They were men of repute. Men who would not wish to have their lives held up to public scrutiny. There were men who had a reputation for ruthlessness, who might be prepared to go to any length to stop the publication of Mrs. Briarton's memoirs, if ever a hint of her "resurrection" and her intention to find a publisher for her diaries, came to their ears.

I thought in particular of an ageing General, still held in the highest esteem, who had been enjoying a night of dalliance with Elizabeth when he should have been on duty. His absence, supposedly because of illness that night, had been responsible for his next-in-command issuing an order for an ill-timed Commando raid on the French coast, in which many lives had been lost.

There was also an old ex-Minister of the Crown who would not dare allow his secret past to be recorded, for the shame it would bring to him, and a wealthy earl, who would be humiliated when the truth of his parentage was revealed.

I shivered uneasily.

Now I understood why Elizabeth Briarton had kept her diaries for those years of her life under lock and key. If a single one of these slim volumes had got into the wrong hands, a blackmailer would have had a field day, making a fortune overnight!

As it was, I thought uneasily, Mrs. Briarton herself could be in trouble, if she published all of this material; could even be in personal danger.

Slowly I replaced the box of books back in the desk, and firmly turned the key.

There was one thing of which I was certain. Mrs. Briarton had been quite right. She did have a best seller on her hands! No publisher to whom she offered her book would turn it down. It would sell like hot cakes. The public likes to think, and even more to learn, that the great have feet of clay, and these diaries told just how many clay feet there were!

One part of me wished I had not become involved in the past life of the woman who had been the notorious Lady Thomis, yet at the same time, I was selfish enough to realise that when these memoirs were published, and sold the world over, as they would be, some of the kudos would rub off on me, and the resultant publicity would do me no harm.

I locked the study door and slowly went up to my room, my mind seething with excitement.

The tame job I had thought I was going to work on had turned out to be as far from tame as a tiger from a household tabby!

FIVE

I came down to breakfast on my first morning at Matfield House bleary eyed from lack of sleep and my head throbbing with tiredness, to find Mrs. Briarton standing at the dining room window, staring out across the snowy waste of the garden, stroking a tabby kitten which nestled in her arms.

At the sound of the tap tap of my high heeled shoes on the parquet floor, she turned round.

"Good morning, Julie," she greeted me with a smile. "I do hope you are not too exhausted after your late night reading session. I couldn't sleep myself, and I saw the light in the study burning into the small hours."

"Good morning, Mrs. Briarton," I smiled back at her. "I must confess I do feel a trifle tired this morning," I managed to stifle a yawn, "but —"

"Yes?" she interrupted abruptly. "But

what? What do you think of my story?"

Her direct gaze challenged me to give a truthful answer.

"Now that you have learned of the kind of woman I was, Julie, have you decided that you would not like to work for me? There is a let out clause in the contract, you know."

She seemed obsessed more with my opinion of her as a person, than with my opinion as to whether what I had read was publishable material.

"Of course I still intend to work with you, Mrs. Briarton," I re-assured her. "Your memoirs fascinated me, as they will fascinate all your future readers!

"I would be a fool to turn down the opportunity to help you with them — for as you so rightly told me — they have all the ingredients for success! They are about an era, the gay Charleston era, which invariably provokes interest, and you manage to bring that era very vividly to life with your descriptions.

"What is more," I met her steady gaze, "you certainly do reveal some scandalous secrets; secrets never even hinted at before about well known people; scandals that will shock and excite the public, and create an interest in your book, making it a talking point!

"Once we have gone through all the diaries, edited them, got rid of the chaff, and given them a continuity, the first publisher you send it too will grab at it, knowing he is on to a winner, but," I hesitated, forcing myself to be practical as well as enthusiastic, "but —"

"Yes?" her eyes narrowed in query.

"I think once we have completed the first draft to our own satisfaction, we should give it to a lawyer to read over to make quite sure you aren't laying yourself open to expensive libel suits, before you offer it to anyone."

"Libel suits?" she repeated. "Why should I be had up for libel? All I wrote in my diaries was true. It all happened! Surely one can't be taken to court for telling the truth!

"There is one thing I must say, though," she went on. "I have no intention of revealing the truth about Toby's parentage, if that is one of the things which is worrying you. Whatever they were, he is a good man, and shouldn't be made to suffer for their indiscretions. For the others, they will just have to take their medicine, nasty though it may taste!"

"It is always best to be on the safe side," I said firmly. "However, the question of having a lawyer vet the book won't arise for two or three months, and in the meantime," I smiled, "I have to admit that I am itching to get down to work on it, and equally agog to glance through all the scrapbooks and photographs and newspaper cuttings in the desk!"

Mrs. Briarton looked relieved.

"Julie, I am so glad that's how you feel about it! I have been on tenterhooks for hours, thinking I might have shocked you so much, you would want to pack your things and go!"

I laughed.

"I am not easily shocked, Mrs. Briarton. Few of us, in this present age, can be, but," my smile changed to a frown, "people of your own generation, even people two or three decades younger than you, might be upset by some of your revelations."

I shifted uneasily from foot to foot.

"This brings me to the one question you may think it impertinent of me to ask."

"Yes?" she snapped.

I hesitated before continuing, and was given a reprieve before putting my worried thoughts into words, by the arrival of Angelina with a tray laden with tea and coffee pots, and a platter of toast, which she set down on the table, before crossing to the sideboard to check that the contents of the dishes on the hot-plate there were all right.

When she had left the room, Mrs. Briarton gently set down the kitten, which had been playing with the gold chain of her lorgnette, and took her place at the head of the table, signing me to take the chair on her left.

"Well, Julie?" she looked at me. "What impertinent question were you about to ask?"

I poked at the fleshy pulp of the pinkish grapefruit on the plate in front of me.

"Mrs. Briarton, have you thought the project through to the end? Have you squarely faced up to the consequences to yourself, which are bound to follow the publication of your life story? Are you quite sure you want the world and his wife to read the details of your past? Do you want the friends you have made here, over the years, as Elizabeth Briarton, to find out that you are also 'that woman' of the scandal sheets, the notorious Lady Elizabeth Thomis?"

It wasn't one question, but several I fired at her in quick succession, pausing for breath before I added, "Yes, Mrs. Briarton, have you thought of all those things? Have you really considered how your life could change? Will your neighbours continue to visit at Matfield, and exchange recipes and garden cuttings and innocuous local gossip over afternoon tea, as has been their wont, or will they cold shoulder you, leaving you to live out the rest of your life as a lonely, perhaps despised, old woman?'

"You don't pull your punches, do you, child?" Mrs. Briarton looked at me with a glimmer of admiration in her eyes.

"I thank you for being so outspoken however, because I believe you genuinely want to save me from my own folly, but yes, Julie, I have considered every point you have made. I have spent many a wakeful night since the idea came to me, pondering all the pros and cons, and what the outcome might be, but I decided, what does it matter what people think of me now. All I want to do is to keep my promise to Charles, and this is the only way I see of making some money to do so.

"I am an old woman, Julie, and not a very strong one. For the short time I have left I can put up with being ostracized, so I am going to try and get my autobiography published, even if I am damned in the process."

"You won't be the only one who will be damned," I retorted wryly. "That General you beguiled from duty, that old Cabinet

Minister, even the holier than thou judge, — they aren't going to enjoy being damned along with you!

"And there is your family," I said. "How will they feel?"

"I have no one of my own left."

"There's Tim!" I pointed out. "He may not be a blood relative, but he appears very fond of you. He might be deeply hurt."

"Tim?" she hesitated.

For the second time since my arrival at Matfield, Tim Briarton's unexpected entry into the room where we were, interrupted our private discussion.

"Did someone mention my name?" he demanded cheerfully.

"I'm sorry I'm late, Liz," he went on, walking up to his great aunt to brush his lips lightly across her forehead in a kiss of greeting.

"As you predicted, the car got stuck in a snowdrift when I was coming back from Morag's. I had quite a struggle to dig it out and get on my way again, and after all the extra exercise I was quite exhausted, and consequently overslept!"

"I did warn you about driving to Ardcraig in the blizzard," said Mrs. Briarton smugly. "You were lucky you weren't stuck in the drift overnight!"

"I wasn't, was I though?" he grinned. "In any case it was worth the risk. The party was most entertaining, and, I almost forgot, Morag thanks you for your present, and she didn't once mention your letter about not selling that land!"

"How is Morag?" Mrs. Briarton asked politely. "She hasn't been to see me for some time."

"She has been very busy, and now she will be busier than ever. You can imagine how delighted she is with all this snow! It is getting the Centre's first winter off to an excellent start. The place is packed with skiers!"

He sat down at table opposite me.

"Do you ski, by any chance, Miss Gilbert?" he asked me. "If you do, how about coming out with me this afternoon? Even if you can't ski, don't worry. It will be nice for you to meet some of the young people at the Centre. Morag is very curious about you," he added with a grin.

I glanced across at Mrs. Briarton and saw her raise her eyebrows although I couldn't decide if her surprised glance was because he had asked me out so unexpectedly, or because of his final remark about Morag.

Certainly each time this name had cropped up, I had sensed that the old lady was not too enamoured of the girl who seemed to take up quite a lot of Tim's time.

Noting my hesitation, Tim said coaxingly, "Come on, Julie," he dropped the formal Miss Gilbert. "You must say yes. I know your afternoons are free. Liz told me so, and you haven't had time to make other arrangements for to-day, so you can't possibly plead a prior engagement!"

"I can plead the lack of ski-ing equipment!" I replied ruefully. "Although Murray — Mr. Sheil," I amended hastily, "said there was a Sports Centre nearby, he gave me the impression it hadn't got off the ground yet, and it never occurred to me to bring my skis with me."

"From that, I gather you do ski then!" grinned Tim. "Now you have no excuse not to come. Morag hires out ski equipment at the centre, and what is more," he added, in a harsher tone, "in spite of Murray Sheil's pessimistic predictions, the Harvey Sports Centre is going to be an excellent one, and that is going to annoy him," Tim added with a malicious gleam in his eyes. "He told Morag and her brother they were throwing good money away with their ambitious concept, and now that they are going to show a profit, he'll have to eat his words, and he won't like that!"

"The Centre is only showing a profit

because Morag was lucky with the weather this winter," said Mrs. Briarton. "If we had had a mild winter, the ski-ing part of the venture would have been an expensive flop! I can understand Murray's concern. He has always been a very careful young man when it comes to giving advice about investments. I only wish that Charles —" she stopped abruptly.

"You only wish that Charles what?" demanded Tim curiously.

"Th-that Charles had lived to see Morag's new Sports Centre," she said blandly. "He always liked to see new ideas come to the fore. It's a pity he didn't live long enough to see you go ahead with his idea of running a deer herd at the Home Farm."

Tim nodded.

"Yes. It's a great pity the Maclellans didn't give up the tenancy a year ago. Then he would have seen his dream become a reality.

"All the same," he went on, pushing his porridge plate to one side, and holding out his cup for me to pour fresh tea into it, "I doubt if Murray would have let him sink money into buying such a herd. The idea still seems too far fetched to him, but maybe I'll be able to talk you into investing some of your money into it, Liz," he chaffed impishly. "I'm sure it would be a gamble worth taking!"

I was about to say something, but Liz shot me a warning look and replied, "I have other ideas for spending my money on, Tim."

"I am sure you have!" he shrugged, "but it was worth a try! However let's get back to our original topic.

"Julie, would you like to come ski-ing with me this afternoon or not?"

"It would do you good to get out into the fresh air, my dear," Mrs. Briarton indicated that she approved of the arrangement. "The mountain air will clear your head, after your late session in my study last night."

"I wondered why the light was still burning in there, when I crept quietly into the house in the small hours this morning!"

Tim shot me a curious look.

"Don't tell me Liz set you to work within hours of your arrival here!" he shook his head and glanced at his great aunt.

"I never thought of you as a slave driver, Liz!"

"Julie sat up late, going over my books, because she wanted to have some idea of what she was about to undertake," retorted Mrs. Briarton. "It was her own wish to do so.

"And Tim," she added reprovingly, "you must stop calling me Liz! You shock Angelina when you do. She thinks you are being impertinent towards me!"

Tim ignored the half-hearted reprimand and winked at me.

"So you were reading the famous diaries last night, were you?" he chuckled. "I know I'm not supposed to know what's going on, but you have dropped so many hints about them, Liz, and what a story they would make!

"Tell me, Julie," he turned to me again. "Did you learn any strange secrets about my favourite girl's past? Are there any skeletons to rattle in her family cupboard?

"I am sure," he went on jokingly, "that no one could always have been so placid and conventional as Liz makes herself out to be. You have just to look into those bright blue eyes of hers to guess she could have been a mischievous youngster! I wouldn't be at all surprised if she had a mis-spent youth!"

I smothered Mrs. Briarton's gasp by saying lightly, "How right you are, Tim! Mrs. Briarton was once the talk of the town, didn't you know?" I laughed.

Tim chuckled, disbelieving the truth, as I knew he would.

"Julie, I think Liz is going to enjoy having you here at Matfield. She needs someone with your lively repartee and light hearted outlook to lean on just now," he was suddenly serious.

Unconsciously he repeated Murray's verdict.

"I think you are exactly right for her," he went on, rising to his feet, excusing himself from table, and giving his great aunt's shoulder a gentle, affectionate squeeze as he stopped beside her chair.

"Yes, Liz," he smiled down at her. "Your idea of getting a companion secretary was not such a foolish one as we all thought!"

He turned back to address me.

"I'll come over from the farm at lunchtime, to pick you up, Julie. The earlier we leave, the longer we shall have on the slopes, so try and be ready for half past one."

SIX

After breakfast, Mrs. Briarton accompanied me to the study, where we sat down to work out my timetable, and to discuss the diaries, so that we could come to some decision about the way to present them to best advantage, either in straightforward extracts, or more in story form.

She explained her ideas on the matter, but told me if I didn't agree with her, she left the final decision to me, since I had more professional knowledge of such matters than she had.

She did suggest, however, that having read the diaries, it might also be a worthwhile task for me to go through all the news cuttings and scrapbooks and photographs to help me absorb the atmosphere of the times, for she considered the conveying of the right atmosphere of prime importance in the presentation of her story.

I had to admire her eye for detail, for her

striving for perfection, when she pointed out a record player on a side table, beside which she had placed a selection of old records of songs and dances of that bygone era, to help me get into the right frame of mind for my task!

Before she left me to get on with the job, she stressed once again the importance of never for a moment leaving the study without replacing every single document safely away under lock and key in the desk.

"Even if you are only going to the toilet, Julie, you must lock everything away! Angelina has been hovering round this part of the house since she learned that I was considering writing this book, and I have already told you what an insatiable curiosity she has about all that takes place here.

"If she were to catch the merest glimpse of one of the diaries or one of the news-cuttings, she would realise I had once been called Lady Elizabeth Thomis, and she wouldn't be able to keep such knowledge to herself. She would tell Tim, she would tell Pino, she would tell her young man at the Sports Centre, and so the news would spread.

"If that happened, Julie, it would be most unfortunate. It could forewarn certain people what to expect, and make life most uncomfortable for me if they wrote to try and dissuade me from writing these memoirs."

"Of course I shall be very careful to lock everything up," I re-assured her.

I sensed that since I had spoken to her before breakfast, she had been re-thinking my words, and was becoming more and more worried and unsure, not so much about what she was proposing to do, as about how Tim and his family, and Pino and the rest of the household, as well as her friends and neighbours in Ardcraig would react when they learned of her past life, and she wanted to keep her secret from them as long as possible.

I could understand this, for in spite of the knowledge I had acquired from reading her diaries, I still found it difficult to associate this fragile, sedate old lady in front of me with the headstrong, notorious Lady Elizabeth Thomis.

Now, studying her face however, I could see, as Tim had pointed out, that a mischievous twinkle still lurked in her eyes. I knew, too, she had a sharp wit which didn't always go with her gentle character.

Further, in spite of the changes time paints in every face, I could see now a resemblance between the woman in front of me, and the youthful beauty who smiled up at me from the photographs spread out on the desk.

At that moment I felt a rising excitement inside me at the thought of the bomb I was helping to prepare; a bomb which would explode myths about so many well known people!

I itched to tell Murray Sheil what a surprise he was in for, and how the dull job he had predicted lay ahead of me was going to be, instead, the most exciting one I had yet undertaken, but I decided against doing so.

It would be disloyal to Liz, as I was beginning myself to call my employer when I thought of her, to give away a hint of her past even to the discreet young lawyer who had selected me to be her secretary, but I couldn't help smiling to myself, after my employer had left me to get on with my work, when I pictured the look on Murray's face when I gave him the final version of the autobiography to read over and check for anything that might be considered libelous or slanderous, before offering the book to a publisher!

I worked hard that morning, and by lunchtime my brain was tired, and I was eager for the distraction that a ski-ing session on the inviting slopes of the nearby mountains would give me.

I was also, womanlike, curious to meet Morag Harvey, whom Tim visited so often, and of whom Liz did not seem to approve.

Although I hadn't expected to ski during my sojourn at Ardcraig, I had expected to do some hill walking and exploring in the area, so I had brought suitable clothes for such expeditions, and the quilted anorak and matching trousers which I donned for my date, made Tim cast an approving eye on me as we walked to his car to drive to the Centre.

"Even if you didn't bring skis, you came well equipped for our chilly winter, I see," he grinned.

"I expect you know, or have been told a dozen or more times, that a girl with eyes like yours should always wear that glorious shade of periwinkle blue!"

"But of course!" I replied, smiling.

He chuckled.

"It is nice to have you here at Matfield, Julie, and not just for Liz's sake! Angelina is bound to find the place lonely at times, with only elderly people in the house."

"You aren't exactly elderly!" I pointed out.

"I know!" he retorted, "that is why she is inclined to haunt me when I'm around, although she means nothing by it," he added hastily. "She has an Italian boy friend at the Centre she sees a lot of during her time off."

"The Centre must be a boon to the young locals," I observed. "It will give them somewhere to go, to amuse themselves. Murray said there wasn't much else in the way of entertainment in this part of the world."

Tim shrugged.

"Murray's ideas of entertainment aren't mine. He's a good skier, give him his due, and an excellent yachtsman, but he prefers the more sophisticated scenes in Switzerland, or Cortina, for his winter sports, and Sardinia or Monte Carlo for water ski-ing or yachting — and of course," he added, "there are no motor-racing circuits near here, and he can't even drive fast along our roads, for they are much too narrow for the speeds he enjoys!"

Something in his tone told me he didn't like Murray, and I wondered why. Possibly it was only the natural jealousy one handsome man has for another, or it could even be that he envied Murray for making an early success of his career, and being able to afford to do all the things he wanted to do, while he, Tim, was still struggling to get his own venture off the ground, and finding difficulty in raising the money to do so.

"Well, Julie," he shot me a quick smile as we drove along. "Do you think you are going to enjoy living here, in spite of the lack of amenities?" he added slyly.

"I'm sure I shall!"

"Liz has certainly taken to you. She also approves of your name. She has a thing about names, you know. I think that's why she doesn't like Morag! She says there's a harshness about the sound, whereas with your name, there is a pleasant softness.

"Julie," he spoke my name again. "Yes, it does have a softness! Were you called after anyone special?"

I shook my head.

"No. I was born in July, hence Julie. My sister was born in June, so guess what!" I chuckled, "She is called June!"

"I wonder what you would have been called if you had been born in February?" he cocked his head at me.

I laughed, amused with his chit chat, and felt a sudden warmth of affection for the smiling young man by my side, who made me feel as if we had been friends for years.

We drove on in silence for a moment or so, then I turned to him again.

"Tim, it must have been a boon for Mrs. Briarton to have your company here when her husband died. She would have been very lonely if she had had no one of her own, in spite of Pino's goodness.

"I understand that she and her Brigadier were very close."

Tim shrugged.

"It was no coincidence that I happened to be here at the time of Uncle Charles's death. He was fully aware how ill he was, and he wanted me to be with his beloved Liz when the time came. He also wanted me to have my final briefings on the schemes he himself had wanted to carry out at the farm, but now he knew he would never be able to do."

"So it came as no surprise to you that you would inherit the farm, when you had been so involved in his schemes?" I spoke rather tartly, remembering, now, how Murray had told me that Tim had deliberately insinuated his way into the Brigadier's good books by pretending interest in the preposterous ideas the old man had had to bring prosperity back to the place.

Tim glanced at me with a puzzled expression.

"Of course not! That was why I always took such an interest in the place, and was so intrigued with my great uncle's very modern ideas about how it could be made to prosper!

"Then, when I knew he was dying, I immediately gave up my job as manager of an Angus farm, to be with him when he wanted me."

"Won't your parents be sorry you aren't returning to New Zealand?"

"My father is dead, and my mother wouldn't expect me to. She knows this is where I have always felt I belonged, and she was very pleased that Uncle Charles and I got on so well.

"He was a great old man, you know. A real visionary, with an eye to fuure developments in the area, and a knack of knowing what was the right thing to do.

"My father often used to say he had a flair for turning dust into gold!

"I only wish," he added ruefully, "he had left me a little of his gold pile, so that I could hurry and get the place in order!

"It is going to take a lot of capital to modernise the building and the outhouses, which the Maclellans let run down, and of course I shall need to build extra high fences round the farm.

"I have toyed with the idea of selling part of the land which runs down to the shore of the sea loch to Morag. Apart from her desire to acquire part of Liz's estate at the mountain tarn, and a right of way across Richmond land, I know she also has her eye on one of my fields which would let her have access to Matfield Bay, where she could promote yachting and swimming facilities for her Centre, but at the moment I know that like me, she is tight for ready cash, and this field comes last in her list of priorities!

"No," he heaved a sigh, "I'm afraid that if the worse comes to the worst and my bank manager won't advance me a further loan, I shall have to try to sweet talk Liz into advancing me a temporary loan, although I doubt if I would get it. I understand Murray holds the purse strings there as trustee of the Brigadier's estate, and Murray and I, as you may have gathered," he grimaced, "do not see eye to eye these days!"

I said nothing, but as we drove along the snow rutted road which now snaked along the cold grey waters of the loch, my thoughts were as bleak as the scenery.

Tim should be told there was no money in the Brigadier's estate. It would worry Liz if he asked her for a loan to advance her late husband's schemes, and she had to say no, without giving him the reason, which her pride forebade her from giving.

Indeed there seemed to be a general shortage of cash among the Briartons and their friends, although as far as Liz herself was concerned, I brightened at the thought, this shortage would not be for long!

It took some twenty minutes to reach the Sports Centre, which seemed to me rather a grandiose title for an old mansion house which had recently been converted into a hotel, with a number of wooden, chalet type huts discreetly hidden by the snow-covered pine trees, to provide extra accommodation.

However, I hadn't time for a good look round, for the moment Tim drove into the car park, a tall woman, in a scarlet ski suit, with a scarlet wool cap hugging her head, came hurrying across the hard packed snow towards us.

"Tim, darling!" she exclaimed, pulling open the door before he had a chance to unfasten his seat belt. "What happened? You are late! In fact, I was so sure you had changed your mind about coming with us to-day, I was actually on the point of going off alone with Roberto when I spotted your car."

Before she had taken in the fact that Tim was not alone in the car, I had time to study the woman's face. Framed by the wool cap and the upturned collar of her jacket, it showed as a perfect oval. The lightly tanned cheeks were smooth and flawless as alabaster, and her large, expressive eyes, under their dark, arching brows, were of a brown so deep they seemed almost black.

Her full, sensuous mouth was painted the same shade as the red of her outfit, as were the nails of the long, slender fingers which still rested on the door handle of the car.

"You didn't expect me to come tearing along here at my usual speed on such an icy road, surely?" Tim smiled up at her before easing himself from the car.

She slipped an arm through his as he stood up beside her.

"Why not?" she smiled at him. "You have always enjoyed taking risks, haven't you? You wouldn't take part in the kind of sports you indulge in if there weren't some element of danger about them, would you?" she challenged him.

He grinned back at her but said nothing.

I got out of the car, and it was only when I slammed the door rather noisily that the other woman appeared to notice my presence. Her eyes narrowed as she watched me walk round the back of the car, to join Tim, who now switched his attention to me, saying, "I thought I would bring Julie along with me this afternoon, Morag," he turned his glance back to her. "She was working till very late last night, and all this morning, so I thought she needed a break in the fresh air."

"Oh!" Morag looked none too pleased. "So you are Mrs. Briarton's new secretary?" she murmured.

"That's right," Tim answered for me. "This is Julie Gilbert, Morag. Julie, this is Morag Harvey, for attending whose birthday party last night, I got myself into Liz's black books!"

I smiled and shook hands, prepared to be friendly with this girl Tim admired, but although she smiled at me, her smile was merely a conventional movement of the lips, and her eyes had a calculating look in them, as if she was weighing me up, and was none too pleased at the result of her calculation!

When she addressed me, I sensed that her words were meant to put me in my place as far as she was concerned.

"So you are the girl Murray selected for his old lady!" she released her hand from mine with alacrity, and once more slipped her arm through Tim's. "I can imagine why. He has always had a weakness for a pretty face!

"But you know," she went on, nudging Tim forward out of the car park and round the back of the hotel, "when Tim told me about you last night, I felt rather sorry for you."

"Sorry? For me?' I gasped with astonishment. "Why on earth should you feel sorry for me?"

"I thought you must have been finding it difficult to get a job in town, if you had to come to a place like this to work," she explained. "I don't suppose you had much choice, really. I believe secretaries or typists or whatever you call yourselves, are two a penny in the city, and interesting jobs are hard to come by."

I could not control the flush of annoyance which rose to my cheeks at her condescending tone, and I had to draw a deep breath and silently count up to ten to overcome my quick flash of anger before I replied, curtly.

"There are always plenty of jobs for competent secretaries in town, Miss Harvey. The demand exceeds the supply. I applied for the position with Mrs. Matfield because I wanted to get out of town!

"I wanted a complete change of scene, with fewer distractions, less of a social life, and a less demanding schedule than my work as fashion editor on a glossie magazine demanded.

"Mrs. Briarton's advertisement appeared

to fill the bill, so I applied for it, and kept my fingers crossed that I would be lucky enough to get it."

Morag was obviously disconcerted by my reply, but she swiftly regained her composure to say, "I do hope you know what you are letting yourself in for. City people often do not appreciate how different living in the country is, until they try it, so I hope you won't find life here not quite what you were expecting, and are disappointed as a consequence."

"I'm sure I shan't be disappointed," I smiled sweetly. "So far, I have found it has more to recommend it than I expected," and so saying I wickedly let my glance rest for a moment on Tim, before looking beyond him at our surroundings.

We had reached the back of the hotel and here I was most surprised to see, only about a hundred yards away, across a broad clearing, a chair lift whose cables stretched up to almost the summit of the high mountain which loomed behind the grey building.

We walked past a group of youngsters whose brilliantly coloured anoraks contrasted vividly with the snowy scene. Some had skis over their shoulders, but others were merely fooling around, throwing snowballs at each other.

"I'm sure Julie won't find life too dull here," said Tim. "There is always plenty to do here, at the Centre."

Morag shrugged.

"Only if you ski, or rock climb, or are fond of the great outdoors," she observed, deliberately making no mention of the après ski ceilidhs and dances which I could see advertised on a board we were passing.

"Julie skis," Tim seemed determined to answer for me. "Unfortunately she hasn't brought her skis with her. She didn't realise she might have an opportunity to use them, but I told her she could hire skis here," he smiled at the girl in the red suit. "That's why she has come to-day."

Morag caught her lip between her small, gleaming white teeth.

"Really, Tim!" she said in an exasperated tone. "I told you we were going to try the Eagle run to-day. It's the first time conditions have been perfect up there for ages!"

She cast an angry glance in my direction.

"We couldn't possibly take a novice up there with us!"

"Perhaps I could give the Signorina some lessons down here, while you and Tim go off to the high run?"

A handsome, smiling-face young man, whose mahogany coloured cheeks spoke of hours spent out-of-doors on the ski slopes, interrupted our conversation.

"That is out of the question, Roberto," Morag said sharply. "You yourself haven't had a chance to try our most challenging run to date, and I insist that you come with us," she spoke petulantly.

"However," she added in a brighter tone, "you've given me an idea!"

She turned to me.

"I shall get one of the other instructors to give you a lesson on the slope over there, if you like," she indicated a small hill where a group of people, mainly children, were being shown the rudiments of ski-ing by a little man in a black ski suit, "unless, of course," she suggested indifferently, "you would prefer to practice on your own on the nursery slopes behind the chalets?"

"The Eagle Run sounds much more exciting than the nursery slopes," I replied blandly. "I wouldn't mind having a go there, provided, of course," I added mischievously, "you can equip me with some decent skis!"

Morag's eyes narrowed thoughtfully.

"I hope you know your capabilities?"

Even Tim looked none too happy at my decision.

"Perhaps we should leave the Eagle for another day," he proposed.

Only Roberto, of the three of them, appeared unperturbed.

"I shall keep an eye on Julie," he flashed me an impudent smile. "And see that she does not get into difficulties."

Tim still looked doubtful, and whispered something to Morag, who shrugged and repeated to me, with a hint of warning in her tone.

"It really is a difficult run, Julie. Unless you are an experienced skier, I wouldn't advise you to come with us."

"I'm not a novice."

"Very well, then, but you can't say we didn't warn you, if you have a mishap."

Morag was right about the skill required for the run, as I found out half an hour later, and although I consider myself more than just a competent skier, it took all of the skill I had acquired in winter holidays spent in the French and Italian Alps, to keep up with the others as we raced downhill.

Morag was as fine a skier as I'd seen in action, and the two men were equally good.

When they all realised that I was not far behind their standard, they stopped casting apprehensive glances in my direction, and we all enjoyed the thrill and exhilaration of the testing run.

Indeed, I enjoyed many exhilarating afternoons on the ski slopes on the days that followed, when my afternoons were free for me to return to the Centre and ski with one or other, or on a rare occasion, all three of that first foursome.

Roberto, the Italian instructor, paid me a lot of attention, and it wasn't only my skiing abilities he was interested in!

Even when we sat in the hotel lounge drinking hot chocolate after a vigorous afternoon on the slopes, his eyes scarcely left my face.

"You fascinate Roberto, because a combination of eyes as blue as yours, and that light brown hair is rare in his part of the world," Morag told me one afternoon when we were walking towards Tim's car.

As the weeks went past, she had become friendlier, because I did not seem to display undue attention in Tim, or even in Roberto, for that matter, and also because she was always able to beat me into second place in the ski competitions in which we took part.

"I hope Angelina doesn't get to hear of his interest," said Tim, unsmiling. "She has a personal interest in Roberto. I believe it was from her he heard about the instructor's job here, and because of her he came here.

"She has a jealous nature, and a quick temper, Julie," he warned me, "and she didn't half give Roberto a telling off at Christmas when he became interested in one of his attractive pupils, and ignored her for a couple of weeks!"

"Angelina is no saint herself!" laughed Morag. "She flirts around as much as Roberto does, as you should know, the way she ogles you, Tim!" she teased.

"All the same, I think you should discourage Roberto, Julie," insisted Tim. "I believe Angelina is serious about him, and I don't want to have Liz upset by a temperamental housekeeper because of a thoughtless flirtation on your part. She is not the kind of person who would appreciate a jealous outburst. Flirtatious rivalries are simply not her scene."

It took an effort on my part to restrain a giggle. If anyone knew about flirtatious rivalries and jealous scenes, Mrs. Briarton did!

However, after this I didn't spend so much time at the Centre. Not because of Tim's words of advice, but because I was becoming more and more immersed in my work, and, now that the snow was melting from all but the very highest slopes, I found I would much rather be getting on with Liz's life story, than attempting to ski in indifferent conditions.

Indeed, I was becoming so involved in the job I had come to Matfield to do, that my original plan of getting down to writing my own novel was thrust into the background.

In comparison with the book on which I was working, the plot I had drafted out for my own book seemed very dull and lack lustre, and no heroine I could have created would have been such a wonderful character as the real life person whose life story I was editing.

Lady Elizabeth Thomis, as revealed by her diaries, was the most fascinating personality imaginable.

She was Scarlett O'Hara, Anna Karenina, The Dubarry — in fact, all the most beautiful and most passionate women of fact and fiction merged into one.

Most of the time, while I worked, I would forget that the notes from which I compiled my material had been written by a woman of flesh and blood, a woman who was still alive!

To me, as the days went by, there seemed to be no connection at all between the wanton beauty of the twenties and thirties, and the fragile, kindly old woman who was employing me to write her life history.

As week succeeded week, I became more and more absorbed in my task, to the extent that I was inclined to give up a number of my leisure hours to completing it, even sitting up late into the night, writing and re-writing and re-arranging my material, changing my mind as to what I should leave out, what would be interesting to leave in, wondering if I was leaving in too much, perhaps, although, apart from the one unsavoury affair which Mrs. Briarton had decisively stated must not appear, she had told me I could include every entry I thought worth while.

Mrs. Briarton was delighted with the interest I was showing in the project.

"You are boosting my morale, by keeping on telling me what a success you are sure the work is going to be," she told me one day, "but apart from that," she smiled at me, "I must confess that I am enjoying having you here. It is so nice to have you to talk to and confide in.

"If only I had had a daughter, or a granddaughter like you!" she added with a sigh.

"There is one thing, though," she went on firmly. "Recently, both Tim and I have been thinking that you are not taking enough time off. You have been keeping your nose to the grindstone all day and every day, and that wasn't in our contract! You will make yourself ill with overwork, and I can't have that!

"In future, my dear, you will stick to the hours we agreed on, and that's that!" she concluded firmly.

I could not get her to understand that I enjoyed working the long hours I did, or the thrill I got from re-creating the people she mentioned in her notes, and whose faces I had come to recognise at a glance from her old photographs and news cuttings.

It was fascinating to put flesh on the bones of her brief entries, and I never felt tired of doing so, even when I worked late into the night.

I tried to explain all this to Liz, but she was adamant that I must stick to the hours stipulated in the contract. To make quite certain that I did this, she took the one step she thought would decisively stop me from overworking.

She took charge of the key of the desk, so that I could only get hold of her diaries when she herself unlocked it, and at the end of my working day, she returned to put them away again, and remove the key!

I didn't want to upset her by further argument, and yet, equally, I wanted to get on with the book in my own way.

I knew my own capacity for work. I knew

I was not overdoing things. I knew that I wrote best under pressure, carried forward on a wave of enthusiasm, and that inspiration cannot be contained in short, set, office hours, and eventually I hit on a solution to the problem.

One afternoon, when Mrs. Briarton had gone to visit friends some distance away, I carefully wrapped the twenty-three slim diaries in polythene, slipped the parcel into a hold-all, and drove to the town, some fifty miles away, where I had confirmed by telephone, that there was a photo-copying service in the library.

Even with seven entries to a page, it was a long and expensive process to photo-copy the lot, but I felt the outlay was well worth it for the time it would save me later on.

How very well worth it this action was later going to prove to be, even I could not have foreseen at that time.

SEVEN

The days seemed to fly past at Matfield, and I enjoyed everyone of them, in spite of Angelina's occasional fit of the sulks, when she got annoyed about something or other. She was very temperamental, and when things went wrong for her, she took it out on me in subtle ways, like forgetting to deliver messages, or accidentally splashing gravy on my skirt when she served at table or, and this I found most irritating of all, interrupting me at my work on some trivial pretext or other.

On these occasions she tried to insinuate her way into the study when I opened the door to her, her curious eyes darting towards the papers spread out on desk and table, but only on the first occasion, when she took me by surprise, did she get more than the merest glimpse of anything, and even then, I doubted if the photographs I had been studying for details of the dresses of the era, would have conveyed anything to her.

Yes. I enjoyed my work. I enjoyed the occasional afternoons when Liz's arthritis didn't trouble her too much and she was able to stroll with me round the garden.

It was a joy to see the snow disappear and the first green shoots push above the rich soil, to develop into golden aconites, drifts of white snowdrops, to be followed by the blues and yellows of the little rockery irises and the more flamboyant daffodils and tulips.

It was amazing to think that the great stretch of garden was maintained only by Pino, and a schoolboy from the village who came only at weekends, and Pino was delighted when I offered to help out with the weeding of the rockeries.

Most of all, however, I found I looked forward to the afternoons I spent with Tim and his friends at the Sports Centre. The ski-ing season had been extended by a fall of spring snow, which maintained the higher runs in good condition, and in a way I regretted the coming of the warmer weather which put an end to these pleasant excursions, and also meant that Tim found more and more to do at the farm, where he now worked very long hours.

However, after dinner in the evening we had time to chat and argue about the many subjects which interested us. Liz enjoyed these evenings as much as I did. She stayed up later than was her wont in order to listen to us, and it was as well, for her sake, for she was supposed to rest a great deal, that my own private work timetable made me excuse myself at nine-thirty each night, when I would retire to my turret suite, not to sleep, but to settle down to work, often long into the night.

Liz would have been angry if she had known what I was up to, but what she didn't know couldn't upset her. As it was, it amused me, as it amused Tim on the occasions he was present, to see what I called the ritual of the keys.

After breakfast, Liz would lead me to the study, where she solemnly unlocked the door for me, and then go in to unlock the desk. I was left in charge of the keys during the day, until half an hour before dinner at night, when I went up to change, she appeared at the study door to make sure I had put everything safely away. Then she would retrieve the keys, lock the desk and the study door once more, and carefully put the keys in her handbag.

Each night, now, when I excused myself

to go to my room, she gave me a smug look.

"I knew you were tiring yourself out with all those extra hours you were spending on my book, Julie!" she nodded knowingly. "A young girl like you needs plenty of rest after working as hard as you do. They say that brain work is much more exhausting than physical endeavour!

"I was right to be firm with her, wasn't I, Tim?" she appealed to her great nephew, who winked discreetly back at me.

His bedroom window, in the main building, was at a slight angle to mine, which was just through the connecting door which led into the turret wing, and he was bound to have seen my light there burning into the small hours, in spite of the thick drapes which I drew across in the evening.

No doubt he thought I was working on my own book now, for I had discussed it with him on a couple of occasions, but at the same time he had no intention of mentioning the fact that I didn't go up to my room to go to bed. What I did with my leisure time was my own concern, and in any case, he would not give me away for fear of upsetting Liz, who was so sure that I was following her advice.

One thing I was very careful of doing was making sure that my copy of the diaries was kept safely under lock and key in my brief case, hidden under a pile of reference books in a suitcase which was also kept locked, when I finished working with them.

Although I tidied my flat myself, Angelina had access to it, to change the linen, and on a couple of occasions I had surprised her leafing through notes of my own novel, which I had left on the bedside table.

If I hadn't been warned of this habit of hers, I had soon learned about it, for she even poked through the dressing table drawers, and tested my cosmetics.

Almost before I realised what was happening, I found I was coming to the final chapter of the memoirs, something which I would never have achieved so quickly if it hadn't been for those long nights of working on the book.

The morning I told Liz I had almost completed the first draft, she was very excited.

"I'm dying to know how you have handled the material, Julie! I am sure, though, that you will have done it just as I would like to have it done, but I'm not even going to peek at the manuscript until you have finished it. Then —"

She stopped abruptly. The smile disappeared from her lips. The glow of delight disappeared from her eyes.

"Oh, Julie!" she shook her head. "Do you know, now that the book is almost finished, I feel quite sad!"

"Sad?" I queried. "You shouldn't be! I am certain it is going to be most successful!"

I frowned as a thought struck me.

"Liz, is it because now the deed has more or less been done, you are beginning to have second thoughts? Are you beginning to wonder if you are doing the right thing?"

"No! No! It isn't that, Julie! My regrets have nothing to do with the book."

"Then what's wrong?" I shot her a puzzled look.

She caught hold of my hand and held it.

"Julie, my dear, you cannot know how much I have enjoyed having you here! It has been wonderful for me, to have someone like you to talk to, to walk in my garden with! I have so enjoyed listening to you and Tim arguing and discussing your young ideas after dinner in the evenings.

"As I told you once before, I wish I had had a granddaughter just like you!

"There is one thing which worries me, though," she went on anxiously.

"I hope you haven't found me too selfish and demanding: too autocratic in my manner at times!"

"Of course not!" I laughed. "Liz, I assure you, I have loved being here! I've loved the work and I've loved being with you. Pino has spoilt me, and Tim has made sure I wasn't lonely when I was off duty by taking me out and introducing me to his friends, and, as you know, my old friends have written to me frequently, and even telephoned from time to time to keep in touch!"

"Murray isn't exactly an old friend, is he?" she teased me, with a twinkle in her eyes, reminding me that her young lawyer had been one of my regular callers, for he had telephoned once a month since my arrival at Matfield.

A flush crept into my cheeks at her tone.

"No," I replied, "but he was only 'phoning me to find out how the work was progressing and to ask how you were getting on. He worries about you, you know."

"He's a dear boy," she nodded. "I never thought he would take his duties as seriously as he does. You know, Julie, he was quite wonderful the way he dealt with Charles's complicated affairs, trying to save me as much trouble as possible. I had so many papers and things to sign, because the estate was entailed, and Charles did not have a direct heir! Half of them were Greek to me, but Murray was so patient explaining everything!"

She shook her head.

"If I had been paid a tenner for every signature I scrawled, I would have been a rich woman!

"Yes," she nodded, "I am glad Murray keeps in touch, especially through you," she added slyly. "I am quite certain he will want to meet you again, even after you leave here, and I hope," she eyed me, blinking rapidly, "I hope I shall see you again too. The doors of Matfield will always be open to you, my dear, if you ever want to return!"

She turned and left the study, and I sat at the table, idly toying with my pen and thinking over what she had said; thinking of Tim and Morag, of Pino and of Roberto, who still attempted to flirt with me from time to time between his flirtations with the younger guests at the Sports Centre.

I smiled, thinking how Angelina now tried to show the young ski instructor that she could play his game, and had started a flirtation with Dave Finlay, a red-haired, freckle-faced, brawny diver, who worked for an oil company, and who was presently spending a month at the Centre Hotel.

Yes, I sighed to myself, I would be sad when the time came for me to leave Matfield. I would miss the gentle way of life here. I would miss the wonderful scenery which I looked out on each day, and I would miss also the pleasant, friendly companionship of Tim Briarton.

However, now was not the time to indulge in such thoughts, I told myself firmly. I still had work to do, and I set to to revise the final chapters. By lunchtime, I had only a few more pages left to deal with.

It was shortly after lunch, when I had gone up to my bedroom to change into my cord trousers, so that I could help Pino weed one of the rose plots, that Angelina knocked loudly on the door.

"Signora Briarton wishes to speak to you in the study," she called to me.

"She says to hurry," she added pertly.

I wondered what could be wrong. Had I forgotten to lock away some document when I had left the room? I was usually very careful about checking, but to-day I'd been excited at the thought of coming so near the end of my work.

I tucked my periwinkle blue blouse inside the waist of my blue cord trousers, and without waiting to put on any make-up, I went hurrying down the turret stairs and along the side corridor into the main hall where Angelina, who had gone ahead of me, stood waiting outside the corridor of the other wing in which the study was situated.

As I approached her, she went to the study to announce my arrival.

"That will be all, thank you, Angelina," I heard Liz say to her. "Thank you for summoning Miss Gilbert for me."

Angelina sauntered slowly away as I entered the little room.

Liz was sitting at the desk, holding the telephone receiver to her ear.

She looked up when I came in and held the instrument towards me.

"Murray has just called me about some business," she said. "Now he would like to speak to you!"

"Oh!" I blushed.

"I'll leave you, then, Julie," she smirked as I took the 'phone from her, "but don't forget to lock the study when you have finished speaking."

"Well, Julie, how are things going now?" asked Murray.

"Murray, everything is going splendidly!" I couldn't contain my enthusiasm. "Since you spoke to me last month, I have got on with the book like a house on fire! What's more, I know it is going to be a winner!"

The lawyer chuckled at my excitement.

"I hope it will be, for your sake, Julie! You deserve a break after this self-imposed exile of yours is over!

"All the same," I could picture the grimace on his handsome face as he spoke, "I sincerely hope, in spite of your natural desire to get on with your own personal best seller, that you haven't let your private interests interfere with Mrs. Briarton's famous autobiography!"

There was a hint of derision in his tone now.

"Remember, you have only two or three more weeks at Matfield to complete the absorbing task you were employed to do, and since you were my personal choice for the job," he went on, "I don't want you to fall down on it, or my old lady might lose faith in my future judgements!"

"Murray!" I protested. "You don't understand! I am not falling down on the job I came here to do. Far from it! It is not my own book that is exciting me so! It's Liz's — Mrs. Briarton's one," I amended hastily.

I giggled.

"I'm dying to see your face when you read the first draft for yourself!

"As a matter of fact, it won't be long before you do, because I have almost completed it, and I don't want to do too much revision until we've had your advice!"

"My advice?" he repeated in a puzzled

tone. "Julie, I'm no literary critic!"

"No, but you are a lawyer," I replied, "and believe me, I think we shall need your help, to advise us if we can reveal all of Liz's past life to the public, or if it would be indiscreet to do so. A number of people are going to be very upset by her revelations!"

There was a pause at the other end of the line before Murray replied.

"Julie, are you trying to pull my leg?" he asked in a suspicious tone.

"Far from it!" I retorted. "Believe me, some parts of her life story are going to cause a great deal of disquiet to certain very well known people, and that's even after leaving out of the book one or two very spicey scandals which appear in her diaries!

"In fact, Murray, if I were to be melodramatic, I'd say that if the original, unexpurgated diaries were to fall into the wrong hands, they would make a blackmailer's fortune!"

"Come off it, Julie!" chuckled Murray. "Now I know you are pulling my leg!"

"I'm not!" I replied indignantly, "and I don't mean a small fortune either! Some of the people mentioned would pay the earth to keep their secrets buried!"

I stopped talking abruptly, my attention distracted by a creaking sound in the hall, as though someone had moved in the corridor just outside the door which Mrs. Briarton had only half closed when she left the study.

I bit my lip with annoyance.

If someone had been hovering out there, they could have overheard my indiscreet chatter!

Still clutching the receiver, I moved stealthily towards the door, to find out who was in the corridor outside.

Unfortunately, the stretched wire of the 'phone caught against an ornament on the low side table as I tiptoed past it.

The figurine was knocked noisily across the glass table top and the resultant clatter must have alarmed whoever had been eavesdropping, if indeed someone had been eavesdropping, for by the time I peered out into the corridor, it was empty.

"Julie! What's wrong? What has happened?" Murray's voice sounded anxiously over the wire. "I thought I heard a crash!"

"I think someone in the corridor was listening to what I was saying!" I said angrily. "When I went to find out who it was, I knocked over an ornament and scared them off!"

"Really, Julie!" Murray's tone was charged with amusement. "I am beginning to think your writer's imagination is working over-time! Scandalous diaries written by dear old Mrs. Briarton and now mysterious eaves-droppers! Are you by any chance trying out the plot of your novel on me?" he chuckled.

"I can just picture you, sitting there under the watchful eye of the Nefertite painting, trying to think up suspenseful ideas to beguile your readers, but the ones you have just tried out on me are much too melodra-matic!"

"Murray, believe me, I'm not trying to pull your leg, and," I bit my lip remorse-fully, "I wish I had never said to you what I did! I promised to tell no one about the diaries in the meantime!

"Oh, dear! I wonder who was listening? It could have been Pino, or Angelina, more likely. She's terribly nosey. I don't suppose it was Tim?" I wondered aloud.

"Julie! You really sound worried!"

"I am!"

"Are the diaries really so drastic?" he asked, with a growing note of interest in his voice.

"You will find the answer to that when you read them!"

"I must say you have whetted my curios-ity!" he chuckled. "Maybe I'll have an op-portunity to wheedle some of the scandalous stories from you when I see you tomorrow!"

"Tomorrow!" I gasped. "Murray! You don't mean you are coming here tomorrow!"

"Some rather urgent business has cropped up in your neighbourhood, didn't Mrs. Briarton tell you about it?"

"No," I replied. "She merely said you wanted to talk to me, handed over the 'phone, and left the room."

"Isn't she a considerate old lady!" Murray laughed. "I wonder what she thought we were going to talk about!"

"Will you be here for long?"

"My business in Ardcraig may take a couple of days, and because she guessed I might have difficulty getting accommodation locally, unless I stayed at the Sports Centre, which I wouldn't want to do, Mrs. Briarton has invited me to stay at Matfield. What do you think of that?"

"I think it was very kind of her!" I retorted.

"I think so too!" he replied softly. "It will be very convenient for both business and pleasure!

"You understand, Julie," he added to my delight. "I am expecting you to take some time off from these absorbing diaries, so that I can enjoy the pleasure of your company again!

"You know what they say about all work and no play, Julie! I don't want to find you have turned into a serious young literary genius!" he joked. "You see, I liked you very much, the way you were!"

"Flatterer!" I laughed. "I'll bet you say something like that to all the girls you meet!"

"Only the pretty ones!" he retorted. " 'Bye for now!"

" 'Bye!" I echoed, adding hastily before I replaced the receiver.

"Murray, please, please don't mention to Mrs. Briarton that I discussed her book with you, or I'll be in hot water. I wasn't supposed to say a word about it to anyone, but knowing you were going to be consulted about it very shortly, I rather jumped the gun."

"Like all good lawyers, Julie," he assured me, "I shall be the soul of discretion!

"Until tomorrow, then, my dear."

EIGHT

I put the receiver carefully back on its rest, but my fingers lingered on it, as if somehow by doing so, I remained in contact with the attractive man I had been talking to.

Right from our first meeting when, after my appointment as her secretary he had taken me into his confidence about Liz's affairs, so that I would fully understand her position, and the reason why I should do my best to produce a saleable product from her memoirs, he made me feel as if he regarded me as someone special; someone he could trust to keep him in touch with affairs at Matfield, so that Mrs. Briarton would not have needless worries about her affairs; someone, business apart, whom he wanted to get to know better.

For my part, I had often thought about Murray while I was at Matfield. Sometimes, when I lay awake at night, I would recall the details of our first, and only meeting. I would remember what he had told me of himself; how he had had to settle for second best in his choice of career because of lack of funds, and how he had accepted the challenge, and made a success of that second best choice, even if he had vague regrets from time to time that he hadn't been able to become a World Class racing driver.

He got these regrets out of his system by buying fast cars, driving them to their limit, and taking part in exciting motor rallies, like the challenging Monte Carlo event.

I admired him because, while still being ambitious, he still found time to think of others and to be kind to his old ladies, like Mrs. Briarton, whom he didn't want to see suffer if he could help it, because of her late husband's lack of foresight in providing for her.

I was thrilled that such a pleasant and attractive man should be interested in me, for he was interested! This telephone call had left me in no doubt about that!

I was smiling to myself, my thoughts still with Murray, when I literally bumped into Tim as I was leaving the study.

I would have fallen if he hadn't caught hold of me to steady me.

He continued to hold me, lightly, looking down at me with smiling blue eyes as he remarked.

"You look as if you are walking in a dream, Julie!"

His touch on my arm was like a gentle caress, and he made no move to let me go.

I was very aware of our closeness; very aware of the fingers pressing gently through the material of my blouse so that I could feel their warmth.

Indeed, for the first time since we had met, I was very much aware of Tim's masculine charm and of the attraction he could have for a woman.

In these seconds of closeness, I could understand why Angelina lingered in the room when Tim was there; why she made a habit of being around when he came back from his work on the farm, darting him flirtative glances from under her long, spikily mascaraed eyelashes, sidling past him with a provocative swing of her well rounded hips; why she somehow managed to brush her slim hands against his shoulder, or "accidentally" touch his fingers when she served him at table.

I could understand, too, why Morag Harvey, so much more sophisticated than the young Italian girl, also found him attractive, and tried to spend a great deal of her free time with him, making a point, while her brother was absent on business, of consulting Tim about the various difficulties which cropped up in the day to day running of the Sports Centre, although most of those difficulties were of such a minor nature, she could have coped with them quite capably on her own, for Morag was no fool when it came to business.

I remembered how, a couple of days earlier, I had remarked to Liz that I was surprised that an attractive girl like Morag was still single.

The old lady had replied with unusual cattiness that to date no one rich enough had come on the scene. In her opinion, Morag was the kind of woman who would not let herself appear to do anything so crude as to marry for money, but she would certainly not marry a man without means, especially now that she and her brother had sunk most of their capital into their ambitious Sports Centre.

"Also, Morag is a woman who likes to get her own way," Liz added. "And this doesn't go down with all men! That is what spoilt her first romance! I must say, though, that I don't like the way she is encouraging Tim. I am sure she is only amusing herself with him. She knows surely, that he has even less capital behind him than she has, and I think she keeps him on her string to make use of him to get certain jobs done for free at the Centre!"

I didn't share Liz's opinion of Morag. I thought she was genuinely attracted by Tim, and at this moment I could fully understand why!

Never had I been so physically aware of a man's charms as I was at this moment. My flesh tingled at Tim's touch. My heart was racing. I was enjoying the sensation of our closeness, though I couldn't understand why, after knowing him for months, I had never felt this way before.

Was it because this was the first time he had held me to him like this; the first time his fingers had caressed my arms?

"A penny for them!"

Tim's teasing voice broke the spell which his hold had woven round me.

Abruptly I pulled myself away from him.

"I'm sorry, Tim. My thoughts were miles away!" I replied shakily.

"Very pleasant thoughts they must have been, Julie, judging from the dreamy look in your eyes! Was your 'phone call from someone special?"

"How did you know I was speaking on the telephone?" I asked, suddenly suspicious.

"I wasn't being psychic, Julie, if that's what you were thinking!" he retorted humourously. "It so happened I was coming to the study to have a word with Liz, whom I understood to be here, when I heard the ping of the telephone bell when you replaced the instrument on the receiver."

His reply was feasible, but it seemed a little too pat, and I couldn't help wondering if he had been the one who had been lingering in the corridor outside the study when I had been so indiscreetly discussing the contents of Liz's diaries with Murray.

At that moment Mrs. Briarton entered the corridor from the hall, and coming towards us, remarked.

"Julie, I am so silly! I was so excited at the prospect of Murray coming to spend a few days with us here, that I quite forgot to ask him what time he would be arriving!

"It wasn't until I was giving instructions to Pino just now, and he asked what train he would have to meet, that I realised I didn't know!

"Did he happen to mention his expected time of arrival to you?"

"He will be arriving late tomorrow afternoon, or possibly the evening. He couldn't give a definite time. He is coming by car, though, so there will be no need for Pino to go to the station to meet him."

"Surely he isn't driving all the way! He will be very tired!"

"It isn't all that far," I pointed out. "About a four hour drive, which will be nothing to Murray!"

While we were speaking of the lawyer's arrival, Tim's attractive smile had changed to a most unattractive scowl.

"What's bringing Sheil up to see you now, Liz?" he demanded in an annoyed tone. "You are surely not having any more difficulties with the winding up of the Brigadier's estate?" he probed inquisitively. "You did mention at one time that you weren't very happy about some things."

"Nonsense! I'm sure I never said anything like that! Murray handled everything beautifully and with the minimum of fuss!

"No, no! His present visit has nothing to do with me or my affairs, although it is a business trip he is making, and a rather tricky business at that!"

Tim cocked his head to one side.

"Which of your friends is in trouble now?" he demanded.

Mrs. Briarton hesitated.

After a moment or two she made up her mind to speak.

"I don't suppose Murray would have

talked to me as he did if he considered the matter private. He is very discreet.

"Actually what he was telephoning me about, was to discuss the Richmonds, or rather their granddaughter. He wanted me to put him fully in the picture, without upsetting the grandparents by asking them too many questions about the child."

"What is he asking questions about Janey Scott for?" frowned Tim.

"Surely you knew she was very ill?"

Tim nodded.

"Yes. Morag told me her little cousin had been sent home from her boarding school in Fife about a fortnight ago, suffering from some peculiar virus illness. But I don't see what Janey's illness has to do with Murray hot-footing it here?"

"Murray's father was the Scotts family lawyer, and now Murray is handling Janey's affairs.

"Mr. Richmond, her grandfather, got in touch with him to-day, to see if he could arrange to release some capital from the girl's trust fund, to pay for medical expenses."

"For medical expenses?" repeated Tim. "I thought all medical expenses were met by the National Health Service?"

"Hasn't Morag told you all the facts about her cousin?" said Mrs. Briarton in a surprised voice, adding, "but then, perhaps she herself hasn't heard the latest developments. She and her brother have barely been on speaking terms with their uncle and aunt, since they were refused permission to allow their clients at the Sports Centre access across Richmond land to get to the ski slopes on Lowth."

Tim interrupted her.

"I thought it mean of the old couple to bar what was always regarded hereabouts as a right of way."

"It never was a right of way, Tim. To make sure it never became one, the Richmonds officially closed the path once a year. I can fully understand their attitude," she went on tartly. "I myself would not want hordes of strangers straggling across my land, in full view of my front windows, every daylight hour every day of the week!

"No! No! It was sheer effrontery on Morag's part to assume she would be allowed access along a private path for her commercial concerns!"

"Morag offered to buy the path and the fields on either side of it from them," said Tim. "The offer she and her brother made was a most generous one — more than they could really afford at the time. Everyone was surprised that the Richmonds didn't jump at it, knowing how the old couple have been hard pressed to make ends meet for years."

"Money isn't everything, Tim, although you youngsters seem to think so these days! The Richmonds value their privacy more than the need for hard cash. It was a pity Morag lost her temper with them when they refused, but that was typical of her!" she grimaced.

"However," she turned to me, "I'm getting away from what we were discussing. The reason why Murray is coming here."

However, she didn't get back to the point straight away, for she digressed once more.

"You know, Julie, some people seem to be born under an unlucky star, and that certainly applies to the Richmonds.

"Once they had a very thriving farm here. Edward Richmond was reputed to have had one of the finest heads of cattle in the country. Then, foot and mouth disease struck in the area, and all his cattle had to be destroyed.

"He was getting on in years. He had no son to succeed him, or help him run the place. He simply lost heart and let things slide. I suppose he thought starting afresh was not worth the effort, and where was the need?

"His only daughter had married Charlie Scott, a very wealthy man, more than twice her age, who doted on her, and would be able to provide for her, so why should he struggle on trying to rebuild his own fortune? He had enough from insurance policies to live in quiet comfort.

"Then, three years ago, Charlie Scott and his wife were killed in a 'plane crash in Madeira. Scott had no relatives, so it was only natural that Janey, his only child, who inherited his fortune, should come to stay with her grandparents.

"There aren't very many children of Janey's age in Ardcraig, so at Murray's suggestion, the child was sent to boarding school in Fife.

"Now ill luck has struck the Richmonds once again. It has now been confirmed that the illness from which Janey is suffering is a very rare blood complaint, for which there is little hope of a cure, although a Doctor Nazareth in Switzerland, who specialises in this particular disease, has recently had some successful cures in his clinic."

"How awful!" I gasped. "The poor child! Do you think there is any hope for her?"

"The Swiss doctor is the only one, but the treatment will be very, very costly."

"At least Janey is luckier than some, in

that she can afford to have the best care and advice," said Tim. "Her father left her a very wealthy young girl!"

"As I said earlier, money isn't everything!" Liz glanced at him coldly. "It certainly didn't bring the Scotts much luck."

"Lucky or not, I wouldn't mind having some of her spare cash to throw around," said Tim. "The renovations at the farm are costing twice as much as I expected," he said in a worried tone, "and I have still to buy the deer herd, and build the deer fencing."

"Health means a lot more than spare cash, Tim!" Mrs. Briarton reproved him. "You have been blessed with it, and with a fine legacy while you were still a young man!"

"I've been lucky, I know," Tim said quickly, adding with a shake of his head, "but I still could do with extra cash. It's easy for you to talk as if money doesn't matter, but you don't know what it is like to have to go begging to your bank manager to plead for further credit! I have sunk all my spare capital into the farm. I just hope the gamble pays off!"

Mrs. Briarton's lips tightened. I could imagine the difficulty she was having in keeping back the retort which would let Tim know that she was far from being the wealthy woman he imagined her to be.

Instead she said, "You aren't the only one who has to beg for an advance! Janey Scott was left a lot of money, I agree, but there were strings attached.

"Charlie Scott was fifty when his daughter was born. He realised he would be in his seventies before she came of age, if he lived that long, so he cannily arranged that the money he left her should be put in a trust fund until she was twenty-five, an age when, in his opinion, she would have learned enough sense to be able to manage her own affairs.

"Janey gets a sufficient income from this fund for her education, clothing and other normal expenses, but she has nothing like the ready cash she will need to pay for this specialist treatment and her stay in the Swiss clinic, perhaps for as much as a year!

"The Richmonds are hoping there is some way Murray can think of to get capital from the trust to pay for the hospital and other fees.

"They wrote to him about this, and after talking to me just now to find out the true state of Janey's health and the grandparents' state of affairs, he decided to come to Ardcraig to discuss the matter, rather than waste time with letters going to and fro.

"In fact," she added in a fond tone, "Murray has even offered to lend them what money they need himself, if it will save them time and stress until the legal side of the estate can be gone into fully.

"Such a gesture is so typical of him," she went on warmly. "He is the most helpful young man I have come across!"

Tim grimaced.

"Sheil is lucky to have capital at his disposal!" he muttered. "He loves showing off about it, too! I am quite sure Morag and her brother, in spite of past differences with the Richmonds, would be willing to help.

"Even I would," he added, "if I had an obliging bank manager!"

I scarcely listened to what Tim was saying.

I was thinking of Murray Sheil, and how, in spite of his outward appearance which suggested a very smooth man of the world, he had a heart of gold.

I looked forward to renewing our acquaintance on the morrow, and to telling him just how much I admired him.

NINE

Conversation at dinner that evening flagged. Normally it is the most protracted and cheerful meal of the day, when Liz and Tim and I talk over what we have been doing and discuss the ups and downs of the day, but tonight my thoughts were far away, and I continually lost the thread of the others' conversation.

I was pre-occupied with thinking about Murray Sheil's arrival the following afternoon. I wondered if I would find him as charming at our second meeting as I had at our first. At the same time, I remembered, with a sudden racing of my pulse beat, the strange sensations I had felt only hours ago when Tim Briarton had held me in his arms.

Surely I couldn't be attracted to two men, and two men who were so different from each other in every way, simultaneously?

I mustn't let my thoughts stray to those moments with Tim, I told myself firmly.

That unexpected tingling emotion I had experienced when he held me was merely a normal woman's normal physical reaction when she is held in the arms of a very attractive man, as Tim's casual caress had been the normal man's normal reflex to holding close a woman he likes. That was all.

Tim and I had developed an affectionate friendship during the months I had been staying at Matfield, but I knew that his interest in Morag Harvey went deeper than mere friendship. That relationship was a different affair altogether, an affair which Mrs. Briarton had told me she wasn't at all pleased about.

In Morag, she saw a lot of what she herself had been as a young girl. To her she was a lovely, ambitious, self-centred woman who wanted to get her own way all the time, and because Liz had a fondness for Tim, she didn't want him to have the unhappy life she herself had made for her first husband.

Resolutely I thrust Tim from my mind and turned my thoughts back to Murray. He was the kind of man I had always admired. He was good-looking, sophisticated, successful, and he came from the same professional background as I did. We had a lot in common, and moreover, I admired the forceful way he went after what he wanted, without quibble.

I smiled to myself remembering how, for the pleasure of my company, he had brushed aside a previous engagement so that we could spend another hour or two together. Moreover, it hadn't been a case of out of sight out of mind, as I had expected it to be, for even though his pretext for 'phoning me regularly here at Matfield was that I could keep him informed of Liz's affairs and let him know if she was worried about anything, so that he could help her out, I knew it was to speak to me rather than to inquire after Mrs. Briarton that he made these calls.

Even to-day, when he had contacted Liz about another business matter, he had asked to be put in touch with me, and from our conversation I believed that he was glad of the Janey Scott affair, which gave him a valid excuse to travel north to see me again.

I hoped he would find me as attractive as he had at our first interview. I also knew I had whetted his interest in Liz's book, although he still thought I was pulling his leg a little in gauging its importance.

I knew, when he learned that what I had said was true, that he would be delighted as I was, that in future the only concern he would have over his old lady's finances, would be how best to advise her to invest the money she would make, and not how to find a way of persuading her she must sell Matfield in order to realise some money to maintain her in relative comfort during her last years.

I was vaguely aware that Mrs. Briarton had addressed some remark to me, and I pulled myself up with a start.

"Julie is day-dreaming again, Liz!" Tim jeered. "It's a wonder she ever gets any work done, the number of trances she has been falling into recently!"

I blushed.

"Don't let Tim tease you, my dear," Liz smiled at me, adding, "I was asking if you still wanted to put in a couple of hours work after dinner, as you asked if you might, since you had taken extra time off to-day. You really don't need to make your time up, you know!"

"But I want to! There is so little left to do, I am excited about getting to the end as quickly as possible, so that I can have your opinion of what I have been doing."

"In that case, I shall unlock the desk again, and get the papers out for you, but please don't work too late."

"I thought if I got the first draft finished

tonight, Murray might have time to cast an eye over it when he comes."

"We'll discuss that later!" Liz said, giving me a warning glance through her lorgnette which indicated that she thought I had spoken out of turn in front of Tim.

"In any case, I doubt if Murray will have any time for my affairs this visit. He will have more than enough to do to attend to all the ramifications of the Scott Trust. It really is the most complicated affair. I don't quite understand all the ins and outs of it, any more than I understand why I was made a trustee of the estate at my age, although I only took over from Charles at Murray's request."

"Angelina," she turned to address the Italian girl, who had entered the dining room so quietly we hadn't noticed her until she had given a discreet cough to announce her presence. "I hope you remembered to put fresh logs on the living room fire," she gave a shiver. "It has turned so cold tonight, and the wind creates draughts everywhere."

"I'd swear there was the feel of snow in the air, which is nonsensical for late May," said Tim, pushing back his chair. "I don't like the way the wind is veering to the north, and growing stronger by the minute," he glanced out of the window to the tall trees which fringed the driveway and which were swaying to one side, as if being pulled over by some unseen hand.

"If you will excuse me," he looked at Mrs. Briarton, "I think I shall go over to the farm and check that all the barn doors have been securely shut. I don't want the wind to go sweeping through them, raising the roofs I have just finished mending!"

"You will have time for a coffee, si, Signore?" Angelina stepped in front of him and smiled up at him. "It is ready. I am just going to the kitchen to fetch the tray to carry to the living room."

"Sorry, Angelina," he smiled down at the girl. "I'm afraid I don't have time for coffee, but perhaps when I come back later, you will brew me a fresh cup?"

She bit her lip with vexation.

"I have a headache," she muttered. "I may not be up when you come back."

"But maybe you will?" he coaxed, and went striding from the room.

Mrs. Briarton looked at his departing figure, waiting until both he and Angelina, who had followed him from the room, were out of sight and sound before turning to me with a knowing look.

"I doubt if Tim has gone off to see his barns. It's more than likely he is off to have a talk with Morag!"

"Why the excuse?"

"Tim likes to keep his affairs to himself, and he wouldn't like me to think that he is worried about Murray's unexpected arrival."

"I don't understand? What has Murray's arrival to do with Tim's keeping a visit to Morag secret? He's never done so before!"

Liz indicated that I should follow her to the living room, where we sat down on the settee in front of the blazing log fire before she continued.

"Yes, I am sure you have noticed he spends a great deal of time with Morag!" she shook her head.

"He makes no secret of it, as I've just said."

"Well, tonight I think he has gone to get things settled between them before Murray arrives on the scene."

"I'm not sure I follow you," I frowned. "Do you think he has gone tonight to see her about the sale of his fields to her? The ones near the shore she is so keen to acquire? Is Murray her lawyer, and do you think he might talk her out of spending the money?"

"I'm not talking about business affairs, Julie, but of affairs of the heart!"

I stared at her in astonishment. What was she trying to tell me?

"I have never discussed personalities with you up until now, my dear, but," she stopped short as Angelina came into the room, carrying the coffee tray, and waited, her fingers twitching impatiently with her lorgnette, until the girl had poured our coffee and handed us the cups before leaving the room.

"You see, Julie," Liz continued when she heard the door click shut. "Morag and Murray have known each other since infancy. Their parents were friends and neighbours, and so it isn't surprising that they saw a great deal of each other. Perhaps what was surprising is that they got on very well together, because they are both very forceful, very positive and yes, I must admit, very self-centred characters! They both like going their own way and getting their own way, and they are both ambitious to make a success of their careers.

"Anyway, they did get on together, and they went around together for years. It was taken for granted by everyone here that one day they would marry, and when Murray was offered a partnership with the Edinburgh firm of solicitors for which he opted to work rather than with his father here, and when later he acquired his father's business as well, he did actually propose to her!"

"And she said 'No', I take it?"

Liz shook her head.

"No, no. Morag accepted his proposal, and the announcement of their engagement appeared in all the local papers as well as the Scotsman and the Times."

"So what happened? They aren't still engaged, I take it?"

"What happened was what should have been foreseen. There was a clash of interests, a clash of wills.

"Morag and her brother have always had this dream of one day turning the Harvey estate into a Sports Centre.

"They have always been sports mad, and good at them all, too, and they realised the potential of the place where they lived.

"If Aviemore could do it, so could they! Moreover, what they were going to offer was something just that little bit different. Something with snob appeal, if you like. They were going to cater not merely for skiers and the general public. They were going to be more exclusive.

"They could offer sailing on the sea loch, with their own stretch of shore; they had their own grouse moors; their own salmon river. They had stables and could offer pony trekking, and there was a loch in the hills for angling, and water ski-ing.

"They could offer all the year round activities, in fact, if they could get their project off the ground.

"They tried to talk their father into the idea. He hummed and hawed, but when he died, not long after Morag and Murray became engaged, leaving his estate between brother and sister, they decided to sink their capital into the venture.

"Murray didn't approve. You know what lawyers are like! They look so carefully into all aspects of a business like this. He thought the scheme would be a flop and that they would never get any return from the capital they invested in it. Such a project, especially the ski-ing side, was too dependent on the vagaries of weather, and a couple of bad seasons could ruin them.

"He advised them to drop the mad idea. He said they had no idea what they would be letting themselves in for, and would end up as paupers!

"Better far, he said, to invest their legacy in reliable stocks and shares, from which they would derive a steady income.

"Morag was furious with him and called him an old fuddy duddy. She said life itself was a risk and she and her brother were willing to accept whatever losses their dream incurred, for the satisfaction of doing what they had decided long ago to do! They argued and argued until in a fit of temper Morag flung her ring back at Murray and told him to give it to someone who would be more obedient to him than she would ever be!

"I think she repented this decision soon after, but she was too proud to say so, and she tries to show her present indifference to Murray by flirting with every eligible male who comes within her orbit. At present Tim is getting the treatment, but tomorrow it could be Tom, Dick, or," she shook her head, "even young Roberto, her handsome ski instructor! It really has been quite disgusting the way she has flirted around since she broke off her engagement!"

I only just succeeded in hiding the sparkle of amusement which came into my eyes at Liz Briarton's forthright condemnation of Morag's behaviour on the rebound to her quarrel with Murray. As far as I could see, the girl was behaving in almost exactly the same way Liz herself had behaved as a young woman, when the man she had loved had refused to let her have her own way!

Mrs. Briarton gulped down her coffee and handed her cup to me to fill it once again.

"All I can say," she went on, "is that Murray had a lucky escape, and I hope Tim will be as fortunate! He is a good boy and a hard worker. Having him here made such a difference when the Brigadier died. He was so kind and loving towards me.

"Come to think of it," she went on slowly, "Tim isn't unlike Charles in many ways. They look quite alike — he's a true Briarton — and he has the same kind and gentle nature, and the same love for their piece of land!"

Liz gave a start as an especially violent blast of wind rattled the window panes and sent clouds of pungent smoke billowing back down the chimney and into the room, scattering blobs of soot over the hearth.

"I do hope this storm abates before tomorrow afternoon," she muttered. "It isn't at all pleasant to drive through the valleys in this area when the wind gusts like this. Even buses have been blown off the road by sudden side winds on the Lowth Pass."

She crossed stiffly to the window and stood there, staring out at the stormy heavens. Black clouds, tinged with fiery copper, hustled across the pale turquoise of the evening sky to shut out the molten rays of the sun.

After a few moments she returned to the

settee, shooting me a sly glance as she sat down beside me again.

"I also hope," she nodded, "that Murray gets his business with the Richmonds over quickly. I certainly have no intention of holding out against any proposal he may make to get capital from the trust to help that poor child get the treatment she needs, so he can count on my signature when he wants it.

"I know he wouldn't mind having some free time to spare for his own pleasure when he is here!" she shot me a knowing smile.

She finished her coffee, put the cup and saucer back on the tray, and pulled the bell sash to summon Angelina to take the dishes away.

The housekeeper arrived with surprising alacrity, almost as if she had been waiting in the hall outside, and as if to explain her promptitude she said in a doleful voice, "Signora Briarton, I was coming to see you, to ask if I could be excused from further duties this evening.

"I have such a migraine!" she sighed, pressing her temples.

"Of course I shall excuse you, my dear! Off to bed with you, and I hope you will feel better in the morning!"

Angelina departed with the coffee tray,

and Mrs. Briarton rose slowly to her feet.

"I shall go up to my room now, Julie," she said in a tired voice. "I feel quite exhausted this evening. Excitement, like this unexpected arrival of Murray, and worry over that poor little Scott child, isn't good for me.

"If you still want to work on the book, as you suggested you wanted to do, I'll leave you to it, my dear," she handed me the keys of desk and study, "but do make sure you don't work too late. I shall keep awake until you return these keys to me, to influence you not to carry on too long.

"In any case," she gave my hand an affectionate squeeze, "you don't want to look tired and bleary eyed tomorrow, do you?"

I walked with her to the foot of the main stairway and then went along to the study wing, but I worked for only a short time before deciding to call it a day.

I was too restless to concentrate on my work. Excitement and tension seemed to be building up inside of me, distracting me from the creative mood.

Moreover, the clamour of the wind which battered against the sturdy walls of the house disturbed me. There seemed to be an eerie overtone to the way it whistled under the eaves and rumbled down the tall, old-fashioned chimneys. Once again a strange presentiment of some impending disaster made me stir uneasily in my chair, and sooner than I had intended, I closed the books, covered the typewriter, locked all the documents safely away, apart from the few pages I had written, a copy of which I put in my handbag, to add to the file I kept hidden in my room, and satisfied all was in order, I pulled out the electric fire from its socket and left the room, carefully locking the door behind me, and slipping the key beside the desk key in my cardigan pocket.

Pino was banking down the log fire in the living room when I crossed the hall to go up to Mrs. Briarton's bedroom.

Seeing me, he called out a cheerful "Goodnight, Signorina! Sleep well!"

I returned the goodnight, thinking that Pino seemed to be the only member of the household who was in normal spirits tonight. The rest of us all had something on our minds, for I doubted if Angelina's plea of a headache had been a genuine one.

True, she had looked flushed and nervy, but I didn't think it was a migraine which had been responsible for these symptoms, any more than it had been responsible for the excited gleam in her lovely dark eyes.

I guessed the headache had been merely an excuse to get off duty so that she could slip out to meet whoever it was I had accidentally overheard her talking to on the kitchen telephone extension, when I'd gone to the staff quarters to give Pino a message from Liz shortly before dinner.

I hurried up the staircase, and knocked on Liz's door.

When she called to come in, I pushed the door open and entered.

She was lying back against a propped up pillow, looking very slight and frail in the enormous double bed, her cheeks almost unnaturally pale in spite of the diffused pink light of the bedside lamp.

She asked me to put the keys in her handbag, adding in a drowsy tone, "I'm glad you didn't work too late, Julie. You are much too conscientious!"

She laid aside the book of Flecker poems she had been reading and continued in a sleep slurred voice.

"I wonder if you would mind filling a glass of water for me, so that I can take my pills? Angelina usually sees to it that I have a carafe by my bedside, but since she wasn't feeling well, she must have overlooked doing so tonight."

I went to the bathroom, filled both carafe

and glass and carried them back to the room.

I watched her swallow her pills, then took the glass from her and laid it on the bedside table.

"You are a very good girl, Julie. A very sweet girl," she murmured. "I have grown very fond of you, you know. When I was in Inverness the other day," she referred to an outing she had gone on with one of her neighbours, "I went to have a talk with Mr. Ogilvie. He was old Mr. Sheil's assistant, you know.

"I told him you were just like a daughter to me and that I wanted — but never mind about that now," she sighed. "One day you will learn what I think of you. In the meantime, let it be another of my silly secrets!"

She patted my hand as I leaned down to adjust her pillows for her.

"Goodnight, Julie, my dear. Sleep well."

I kissed her lightly on the forehead.

"Sleep well yourself, Liz," I said softly, and switched off the bedside light before quietly leaving the room.

She was already snoring gently by the time I reached the door, which I closed very softly behind me.

I was glad I hadn't worked as long as I had meant to, for Liz would have been over exhausted had she persisted in keeping awake for me. As it was, I had never seen her look so tired and frail.

I thought of trying to find my way to the turret wing from the floor I was on, but there were too many corridors, and rather than seem to be prowling about, I returned to the main hall, and went along the corridor to the spiral stair which led to my suite of rooms.

At this side of the house the wind seemed even noisier, and it wailed like a lost soul through the loosely fitting window frame, making me shudder uneasily, afraid the glass might give way before the blast.

I lost no time in getting into bed, where I pulled the bedclothes over my head, to deafen the tormenting scream!

TEN

Tired though I was, sleep evaded me. I tried everything I knew to woo her, but all in vain. I tossed and turned. I heard each creak and groan of the old house, creaks and groans to which I had become accustomed over the months of my stay at Matfield, but tonight, along with the noises which I recognised, there were other sounds; sounds whose origins I couldn't place; sounds which could have been caused by the gale sweeping through each nook and cranny; stealthy rustlings as if someone was creeping furtively along the corridor; then a brittle sound, as if a pane of glass in one of the downstairs rooms, far distant from the room in which I was lying, had shattered.

I sat up with a start at this noise, but was reluctant to get out of bed to investigate it.

If Tim had returned from his visit to the farm, I would have made my way to his room to tell him I thought the gale had blown in one of the windows, but as yet I hadn't heard him come back, and I was now convinced that what Liz had suggested had been correct.

He had used the possible effect of the gale force winds on his barns as an excuse to visit Morag that night, to ask her to marry him before her former fiancé returned to Ardcraig.

Was Morag still interested in Murray, I wondered, and vice versa. Was he merely pretending an interest in me, knowing she was bound to hear of it, in order to let her know that he could dally with someone else as well as she could?

I moved restlessly under the covers, and didn't finally settle to sleep for another ten minutes, shortly after I had heard the clunk of Tim's bedroom door as he pushed it shut, for although his bedroom was in the main building, the way the turret had been built, our bedrooms adjoined at a slight angle, and I could always tell, by the creaking of the floorboards, when he was in his room.

My sleep was fitful, however, and I stirred every few minutes, roused by the gusting wind which made the windows rattle.

The third time I was wakened however, it wasn't the noise of the wind which made me sit up uneasily. There was something else which stirred my senses, telling me something was amiss, but what it was I couldn't decide, until I inhaled a long, sleepy breath as I stretched and yawned, prepared to lie down again.

Now I realised that what had troubled me was the smell of smoke and the odour of burning wood.

Still sniffing, I flung back the bedclothes, got out of bed and hurried across the room, to draw aside the curtains and peer out of the window.

I still wasn't particularly perturbed. This was the season of gorse fires on the hillsides, and I vaguely thought that the wind was blowing the smoke from these fires in the direction of Matfield.

Ahead of me I could see nothing but the dark outlines of the garden trees, and further away, the dark mass of mountains against the night sky, with not a single line of flame running along their ridges to show that the gorse was burning.

Yet the smell of smoke was getting stronger, and now, as I stood there, I could hear a crackling sound; the crackling sound that a log fire makes when it is blazing vigorously.

A shiver of anxiety shook my body. I opened the window and leaned as far over the sill as possible, to look up and down the façade of the house. I gazed first towards the far away turret wing which, like the one in which I had my suite of rooms, stood slightly proud of the main structure.

To my dismay, I saw smoke pouring from the window of the study on the ground floor, and a ruddy glow was reflected on the panes of glass.

Even as I watched, another pane of glass cracked with the heat, and more smoke came billowing out into the night, while the flames, fanned by the stream of air which the high wind forced through the break, leaped up with violent orange tongues.

Without taking time to put on slippers or to pull on a housecoat, I went rushing from the bedroom, shouting a warning which I hoped Tim would hear as I pushed and pushed at the door, at right angles to my bedroom one, which Pino had pointed out to me on my arrival, telling me it led to the central block, should I need to get there in an emergency.

The door seemed to be jammed, and it took a considerable amount of shoving to open it. When I managed to do so, I hammered on Tim's bedroom door, which was just on the other side of the connecting one, shouting shrilly,

"Tim! Tim! Wake up! The house is on fire! Get up! Get up!"

I waited until I heard him call back before I went racing along to the top of the main staircase, and past it, to Mrs. Briarton's bedroom.

Tim came racing after me.

"Julie! What's happening! You were shouting 'Fire'!"

"The other turret wing is on fire," I called to him. "I could see from my window that the study was well alight!"

He wasted no time in asking further questions.

"We'll have to get Liz out of the house," he said, pushing open the old lady's bedroom door. "She will probably be so drugged with the pills she has to take to make her go to sleep at night, she won't wake up, and I shall have to carry her.

"Julie, you run and warn Angelina and Pino, and then call the fire brigade. I shall carry Liz out to the summer house."

I turned to do his bidding, only to run into Pino who was rushing up the stairway.

"Thank God you are all awake!" he gasped. "I have already telephoned for help. It was Angelina who warned me! She saw the fire when she was coming up the drive," he gasped, hurrying towards his mistress's bedroom, to give Tim a helping hand with the old lady.

I stood for an irresolute moment, shivering in the cold air, and now very conscious of the very skimpy nightie I was wearing. In spite of the emergency, even Tim noticed my trembling and said gruffly, "Julie, we'll get Liz out all right. Your room is a good way from the blaze, and I think you should dash back there and get some warm clothes on, and bring some extra blankets to wrap round Liz."

I did as I was told, and it didn't take me more than a couple of minutes to pull on a pair of trousers and a warm pullover and grab the covers from my bed. I even took a precious minute to stuff my brief case and handbag under my arm. I knew the flames must have destroyed Liz's original diaries, but I was damned if, after all the work, and all the hopes Liz had had for the publication of her memoirs, the copies I had made both of the diaries and of my draft book, should go up in smoke with the originals!

By the time I rejoined Pino and Tim and Angelina, who was still fully dressed, they had almost reached the summer house which lay at the far end of the rose garden.

We could already hear the distant clanging of the fire bells and the sirens of the police cars as they raced towards Matfield.

"I hope they get here in time to save the main building," muttered Tim. "As it is," he looked down with a worried look at the old lady who still lay asleep in his arms, "the shock of what is happening to her beloved house might be too much for her."

He heaved a worried sigh.

"The doctor has warned her against undue excitement. I expect you know, Julie, that she has a weak heart," he added. "This could put too much of a strain on it."

"I have the Signora's pills here," said Pino, who had taken the extra blankets from me. "Perhaps if she remains asleep for a time — if she does not see the flames and hear all the stirring noises, the shock might not be so great."

"She is bound to wake up with all this clamour!" groaned Tim as the din of the approaching cavalcade grew louder and louder.

Even as he was speaking, Liz stirred in his arms. Her eyes fluttered open for a moment, and gazing up into the face of her late husband's grand nephew she whispered, "Darling! My darling Charles! I knew you would never leave me!"

The pale lips softened into a contented smile as she looked at Tim.

He looked down at her with affection in his gaze.

"Yes, I am here with you," he replied softly, "So go to sleep, my love. Go to sleep!"

"Dear Charles!" Liz smiled contentedly. Her wrinkled eyelids closed over her blue eyes. She breathed a slow, deep sigh, and relaxed once more into a deep sleep.

Pino looked with affectionate eyes at the younger man, nodding his approval of the deception as he trotted alongside Tim and his burden.

Although it was May, the strong, fresh breeze made the air distinctly chilly, though no doubt the firemen, already plying their hoses on the blaze, would not have agreed with me.

Wrapped in her blankets, held close in Tim's strong young arms, Liz wouldn't feel the cold either, I thought. It was odd how she always seemed to have had a man to comfort and care for her, from her first husband, through a succession of lovers, to the Brigadier who had cossetted her for over thirty-five years, then Murray who did his best to cushion her against her monetary losses, and now Tim.

I felt an unreasoning stab of jealousy, watching him smile down at her as he was doing, noticing the tenderness with which he held her and with which he laid her down on the emergency bed which Angelina had prepared in the summerhouse.

For the first time I noticed his resemblance to the photo of the old Brigadier which stood on the bedside table in Liz's room. They both had the same rugged features, the same clear eyes, the same heavy brows, and, I hazarded a guess, possibly the same mannerisms, the same kindness of heart.

It would be nice to be loved by such a man, I sighed. With him, I guessed love might come before ambition.

"Julie!" Tim turned round to speak to me. "You and Angelina stay here with Liz," he ordered. "Pino and I will go and see if we can salvage anything from the wing."

His lips tightened into a grim line as he glanced towards the house.

"We have been lucky, in a way," he said. "If Angelina hadn't sneaked out to see her boy friend and stayed out so late, and if Pino hadn't been waiting up for her to return, as he always does, things might have been a great deal worse. A great deal worse," he repeated, shooting a grateful glance at the two Italians.

"Yes, if you two hadn't been up and about, and sent for the fire brigade so promptly when Angelina spotted the fire, the whole house could have gone up in smoke!

"But we can't stand here talking," he took hold of my arm. "Julie, you just make sure that you stay with Liz, all the time, in case she wakes up again. If she does, you and Angelina must re-assure her that things aren't as bad as they could have been."

"Signor Briarton!" Angelina caught at his hand. "The poor Signora! How can we console her when she wakes and finds out what has happened! All her memories were in that room!" she gestured towards the study which was hidden from us by a pall of smoke. "All her memories," she repeated, "and all the lovely plants in the orangery next to it, which she tended so carefully, since each one was a special gift from her husband — they will all be burned to ashes now — her plants, her souvenirs, her diaries, even the book she was having written about her life!" her words were choked by a sob. "Yes, all of it has been lost there! Her memories, her past happiness —"

Angelina's fingers clutched at Tim's fingers and her voice rose into a hysterical wail.

"When she learns what has happened, it will kill her!"

She turned to gaze distractedly at the old

woman who slept on, blissfully unaware of what was going on around her.

"It will kill her!" she repeated. "She has a bad heart! She will not stand up to the shock!"

"No, Angelina!" Tim spoke briskly. "Liz will be all right. She has stood up to misfortune before now. She will come through this one, but she will need your help. So please," he smiled at her encouragingly, "Don't let her down. Stay with her. Comfort her if she wakes up."

He pulled himself free of her clasp and went hurrying after Pino.

I felt so useless, standing there, unable to do anything but gaze compassionately down at the frail figure on the emergency bed.

Tim had said Liz was tough, but how tough do you have to be to survive one major tragedy after another within a short space of time?

Like Angelina, I dreaded that the shock of what had happened this night might prove fatal, for Liz had looked far from well when I had said goodnight to her in her room scarcely three hours earlier.

It seemed ironic that now, when there was a possibility that she would be able to pay for the maintenance of Matfield for as long as she lived, her dream should go up in smoke.

Angelina bent forward to tuck the blankets more closely round her mistress, and hovered over her in a way which indicated that she, rather than I, had been left in charge of the old lady.

I stepped back a pace, and glanced towards the house, relieved to see that already the fire had been brought under control, and that the only damage done by the flames and the water from the firemen's hoses, seemed to be confined to the one wing.

I couldn't think how the fire could have started. There were no open fires in that part of the building. No one in the house smoked, so it couldn't have been caused by a smouldering cigarette butt.

Certainly I had used the electric fire in the study for the hour I had been working there, but I had been careful not only to switch it off, but also to pull the plug from the socket before I left the room and locked it up for the night.

Liz stirred in her sleep, and at her movement I bent forward to take one of her hands gently in mine, and hold it tenderly.

For all her gaudy past, I had grown to love this gallant old lady who had been so determined to carry out her beloved husband's last wish, even if, in finding the means to do so, she became an outcast from her circle of friends.

At my gesture, Angelina drew in her breath in an angry hiss.

"How can you act like this! How can you behave so calmly, when you are the one who is responsible for what happened!" she flared at me.

I gaped at her.

"What do you mean?"

"You! It was you who started the fire, Signorina Gilbert!" she rounded on me angrily. "You and your carelessness are responsible for all that damage!" she gestured towards the house.

"Don't be silly, Angelina!" I gasped angrily. "I had nothing to do with it. I was asleep when the fire started.

"Asleep?" she sneered, her malevolent gaze taking in the fact that unlike Tim, I was not in my sleeping apparel but fully dressed.

"You were in the study only minutes before the blaze started! I saw you! I was standing near the orangery, where the driveway sweeps round to the back of the house, and I spotted you in the study, leaning over the desk!"

"Rubbish! I certainly wasn't there less than half an hour ago! I was in my room! I went to bed early! And in any case," I added, "You couldn't have seen into the study, because I had left the curtains drawn over the window!"

"You were there!" she persisted. "The window was open, and the wind had blown the curtain a little to one side, and I could see someone — you — leaning over the desk.

"You can't deny you were working late. You said you would be, but I didn't think you would still be there when I returned, so when I saw you, because I was afraid you might see me, and report to the Signora I hadn't gone to bed as she thought, but had gone out, Dave and I walked back down the drive again, and I didn't come back for another ten minutes, when I tried to sneak past in the shadow of the trees.

"That's when I smelt the smoke coming through the open window. I ran up to the window, and I could see papers scattered all over the place. They were already burning, as was the desk and chair beside it. Then all of a sudden the curtains went up in flames, and that was when I ran to get hold of my uncle!

"So you see," she rounded on me viciously, "you can't talk your way out! I saw what happened! You had left papers scattered around. You must have forgotten to switch off the fire, and the draught through the open window blew the papers against the element, and started the blaze!

"Yes, Signorina Gilbert, you can't deny it! You started the fire, and if my poor Signora dies as a consequence, I shall never forgive you, never!" she declared, bursting into tears.

ELEVEN

Angela's accusing tirade left me speechless. I stood there, still clutching Liz's frail hand, gaping at the angry girl in dismay.

Pino's return broke the silence.

"The men have already got the fire under control!" he announced. "Thanks to God, the damage was confined to the study, and now, apart from smouldering floorboards and pieces of furniture, it is almost out!" he breathed a long, relieved sigh.

"It's Angelina we have to thank!" said Tim, who had followed Pino.

He smiled at the flush-faced girl.

"There is no doubt that your early warning saved the house! The firemen tell me that if they had arrived even ten minutes later, the flames would have spread to the rest of Matfield! As it is, they tell me we should be able to get back into the house quite soon, although they intend to leave one of their fire engines standing by for

179

another couple of hours, in the remote chance of a renewed flare up."

He moved up to the bed where Mrs. Briarton was lying.

"We may even be able to get Liz back into her own bed again before she wakes up! Then we would be able to break the news of what has happened tonight without over-upsetting her. If she wakes up to find herself out here in the middle of the night, and sees all the hustle and bustle and the fire engines, the shock might be too much for her," he shook his head anxiously.

"Thank God Matfield has been saved!" I said softly. "If it had been destroyed, she would have been too, there is no doubt of that!"

"And it would have been your fault!" Angelina flared at me again.

She turned to the others, repeating her accusation.

"It was the Signorina Gilbert who was responsible for the fire! I saw her in the study only minutes before it started!"

"Impossible!" ejaculated Pino. "The Signorina went up to her room not long after ten o'clock! You couldn't have seen her in the study!"

A movement from the old lady on the bed distracted him.

Liz opened her eyes and stared up at us.

"What's wrong? What are you all doing here?"

For the moment she seemed unaware of her surroundings, but as she struggled to a sitting position and looked about her she gasped.

"What am I doing here? What has happened?"

With unexpected vigour she pushed me aside, and now she had a clear view through the door of the summerhouse, across the rose garden, to Matfield, where, in the pale golden brightness of the early dawn, the sun's first rays reflected back from the scarlet fire engines and the blue lights on the roofs of the police cars which were drawn up in front of the building.

"Matfield!" she cried shrilly. "Matf—" the word slurred to silence; the wrinkled mouth moved, but no sounds came from it as she sat, paralysed with shock, staring at the scene.

"Will it be safe enough to take her back indoors?" Tim turned anxiously to the firemaster who had just joined us.

"I came to tell you you could go back to the house," he nodded.

"Then, Angelina, you go and telephone Dr. Boyd," said Tim, taking charge of the situation.

"Julie, you get her bed ready for her. You will need fresh blankets. These ones she is wrapped in are quite damp with the night air.

"Pino! Help me carry your mistress back indoors!"

We all automatically obeyed his authoritative orders. For me, it was a relief to have something definite to do.

We settled Liz comfortably back in her own bed. Dr. Boyd came and spent some time with her while Tim and I waited anxiously in the living room for his verdict.

"Mrs. Briarton is gravely ill," he told us. "She may not have told you, but her health has deteriorated greatly of late. This often happens to an elderly person after the loss of someone they have loved dearly. I told her she must take things easy, but in spite of my pleas she continued to do more than she should. She said there was a job she wished to finish before she died, something about a book," he shot me a curious glance.

"Now this, on top of her decline, isn't very good," he pursed his lips. "With luck we may pull her through, but she must be kept very quiet and have no excitement at all!"

He glanced at Tim to see if he approved of his next suggestion.

"I think I could persuade Mrs. Campbell to stay with her for the next week or so. She is a retired nurse, and would be capable of dealing with any emergency. I noticed a dressing room next to Mrs. Briarton's room. She could sleep there."

Tim agreed, and the doctor left to make the necessary arrangements. As Tim was showing him out, the firemaster and the local police sergeant arrived.

The fireman stated the reason for his visit without wasting words.

"We have reason to believe that the fire in the study was started deliberately!" he shocked us by announcing, and added the reasons for his conclusions.

"That's nonsense!" said Tim. "Who would want to do a thing like that? In any case, how can you be so sure the fire was not an accident? There could have been a short circuit, something like that."

"I'm afraid not," the man shook his head.

"But there was no one in the study for some time before the blaze started," said Tim.

"She was!" reiterated Angelina, who had been up to her old game of eavesdropping on our conversation.

She came storming into the living room, pointing an accusing finger in my direction.

183

"She was!" she said again. "I saw her, I don't care what uncle says! Ten minutes before the fire started, I saw her in the study, leaning over the desk, examining papers."

"That's a lie!" I retorted angrily. "I went to bed before half past ten!"

"No! You were there!" she shrilled. "Dave can confirm what I say!"

"No," said Tim firmly. "Dave couldn't confirm that, because Julie went up to her bedroom just as I arrived back at Matfield last night! I saw her walk along the corridor towards her suite —"

"It's true, Angelina," put in Pino. "The Signorina said goodnight to me when I was banking up the fire in the living room. Seconds later the Signor Briarton arrived, and we stood in the hall talking for some time. Then the Signore asked if I would make a pot of coffee for us, and we were there, together, in the living room talking about the work he had been doing on the farm that day for some considerable time."

"Yes," nodded Tim, "and when I went up to my own room after that, I could hear Julie in hers. The springs of her bed creak when she turns in it," he shot me a reassuring look, "and also," he grinned suddenly, "she snores!"

"I do not!" I cried indignantly. "In any case, I was awake when you came to your room. I heard your door shut."

"But someone was in the study!" Angelina stated positively. "We saw her — him! Whoever it was was leaning over the desk, looking at papers, scattering them about, pulling things from the drawers! It was only a glimpse we got, through the chink in the curtains, but I," she bit her lip, "I naturally assumed it was the Signorina who was there. She is the only one, apart from Signora Briarton, who is allowed into that room!"

The police sergeant looked at the fireman, and then at us.

"There have been a number of break-ins in the neighbourhood recently. Young campers running short of money and food; hikers, the odd tinker, and such like," he nodded. "Often when they don't get what they want they resort to spiteful vandalism, breaking things up, ripping curtains, smearing dirt over walls, that sort of thing, but to date they haven't set fire to anything."

"There was nothing in the study which would have been of value to a casual thief," I said. "Only papers and books and family photographs, apart from one or two pieces of antique furniture."

"So obviously in their indignation at not finding what they wanted they heaped the papers and furniture round the desk, and set fire to the lot!" said the fireman grimly.

"It's over to you now, Sergeant, to make further inquiries!"

The rest of the morning was spent answering police questions, discussing the affair with each other, worrying about Liz, arranging the room for Mrs. Campbell, and dealing with a constant stream of visitors who came to inquire after Liz.

After lunch, Pino and Tim spent some time tidying up the one-time orangery, adjoining the study, which Liz had made into a plant house for the rare specimens she collected. Some of the plants had been damaged by smoke and water, but the majority of them had survived.

I sat in my room, and carefully revised the final chapter of Liz's memoirs, so that it would be ready for Liz to read over when she was able to do so, and then we could get it off to a publisher as soon as possible.

If Liz had been in need of money before, to keep her house up to standard, she would need it even more now, to help put to rights the damage which the fire had caused to the right wing.

I had at least one thing to feel cheerful

about. If I hadn't surreptitiously had the diaries photo-copied, and made copies of all my notes, and of the book I was working on, all Liz's dreams of making money from her memoirs, and all the hard work I had put in these past months would have gone up in smoke, for it had been impossible to salvage any of the precious documents from the almost completely burnt out desk in the study.

Knowing that her book, and her diaries still existed, even if not in their original form, would be a boon to Liz, and I determined, at the first opportunity, I would make another copy of the copies, just to be on the safe side once again!

I finished my work, and put the papers safely away once again, before making myself a cup of tea in my little kitchenette.

I stood at the turret window, drinking my tea, and looking out at the garden stretched out below, and across the sea loch at the foot of it, to the mountains beyond.

Far to my right, I could glimpse the roofs of the houses in Ardcraig, and the road which snaked from the village, along the waters' edge, losing itself among the trees which marked the boundary of the estate, and then reappearing alongside the fields.

There had been more traffic on the road

between Ardcraig and Matfield to-day than there had been in all the months I had been here.

Apart from the firebrigade vehicles and the police cars toing and fro-ing, there had been a steady stream of cars conveying friends and neighbours to Matfield to learn the latest news of Mrs. Briarton, and wanting to know if there was anything they could do to help.

Angelina had made endless pots of coffee and I had poured out countless cups of the scalding liquid since shortly after breakfast, to hand to these visitors.

Tim had automatically expected me to assume the role of hostess and receive the callers with him, and even Angelina seemed to accept me as deputy mistress of Matfield.

Fortunately by lunch-time the stream had dried up, but now as I glanced at the road, I noticed a dark coloured car speed along in the direction of Matfield, followed minutes later by another car whose gleaming red reminded me with a shudder of the fire engines.

When the first car came to a halt almost directly below my window. I recognised it as Morag's.

As she got out of the car, she looked up and seeing me at the window, waved to me.

With a sigh, appreciating that I would have to go down and talk to her, I finished my drink, washed the cup, and hurried down the spiral staircase.

By the time I got down to the main hall, Morag was walking towards the living room, arm in arm with Tim, and they sat down side by side on the settee, talking in low voices.

They looked round when I entered the room.

"I would have called sooner, Julie," said Morag, "but I knew you would be inundated with visitors this morning.

"What an awful thing to happen! It's a wonder Liz didn't die of shock right away when she woke up and found her beloved house was on fire! How is she now?"

"Still sedated," I replied.

"Tim must have been glad to have you on the spot," Morag's voice was friendly. "I don't expect Angelina would be of much help! No doubt she was having hysterics all over the place," she added with a note of malice in her tone.

"Angelina was most helpful," said Tim, "and far from hysterical. She has been coping wonderfully with all our visitors and with the police inquiries!

"It's been some day, believe me, and as

you have just said," he sighed. "I was glad to have Julie to help me."

"Is there anythhing that I can do?" asked Morag. "Not that I expect there is. You seem to have everything under control, and —"

She stopped short, interrupted by the clangour of the front door bell.

Tim grimaced.

"I don't think I can face another kindly old dear coming to ask after Liz! They mean well, I know, but it can be tiring making polite conversation and saying the same things over and over again!"

There was a knock on the door and Pino came in to announce.

"Mr. Sheil is here!"

Morag let out a surprised ejaculation.

"How on earth did he get here so quickly? Did you send for him?"

"I'd completely forgotten he was coming!" I gasped. "Tim! We should have got in touch with him, and told him what happened!"

Before Tim could reply, Murray came into the room, smiling.

"I hope I haven't arrived too soon," he said. "Pino seemed a bit put out when he saw me!"

"What did you expect him to look like, after what has happened here?" said Morag curtly.

"What do you mean?" said Murray shooting a bewildered look at us.

'I'm sorry, Murray," said Tim, "we should have let you know what happened, but there was so much else to think about, your arrival slipped from our minds."

Murray looked even more bewildered, and turned to me appealingly.

"Julie! What's wrong? What's been going on here?"

"Matfield nearly went up in flames last night, that's what's wrong!" snapped Morag. "Now Mrs. Briarton is at death's door with the shock!"

"Good God!" ejaculated Murray, his eyes looking as if they would pop from his head. "Why didn't someone tell me!"

"Because, as Tim said, the fire put everything else from our minds!" I replied.

He leaned against the back of my chair.

"I can't believe it! Matfield on fire!"

He looked around him.

"I don't see much sign of damage!"

"That's because the blaze was spotted before it could really get a firm hold. Damage was confined to one wing, in fact mainly only to the study, but as you can imagine, there was a bit of panic at the time, and when Liz realised what was going on, she collapsed."

Murray looked shaken.

"Is there anything I can do?"

"Everything is under control now." Tim shook his head.

"I don't expect you will want me to stay here now," Murray bit his lip.

"What brought you here in the first place?" Morag's curiosity made her butt in.

"I am here to see your uncle, Morag. We have things to discuss about Janey. It's all very complicated and could take some time. That's why Mrs. Briarton said I could stay here for a day or so, until we got the legal tangles unravelled."

"There's no reason why you shouldn't still stay here," said Tim slowly. "Liz told Angelina to prepare a room for you yesterday, so you might as well use it."

"Are you sure?"

"Why not?" shrugged Tim. "It's not as if you came here on a social visit and expected us to entertain you!"

While he was speaking, Angelina came into the room carrying a tray with coffee and biscuits.

"My uncle thought you might need this after your long drive," she ogled Murray.

"Pino was quite right," he smiled at her. "The twisty roads around here make for tiring driving!"

While we sipped our coffee Murray asked for more details about the outbreak, and was taken aback to learn that the police suspected that it had been started deliberately.

"How can they tell that?" he asked incredulously. "You would think any evidence of that kind of thing would have gone up in smoke!"

"That's the layman's idea," said Tim, "but it is surprising what the experts can sift from the ashes!"

"But who would want to set fire to the place? Liz would be the only one to benefit, from the insurance, and she loved Matfield too much to destroy it for its money value!"

"Of course Liz wouldn't do such a thing!" I was taken aback at the suggestion, "but someone certainly did, and it was without a doubt the person Angelina saw in the study not long before the outbreak. She thought it was me at first!" I flashed Angelina an indignant glance, still smarting at the thought that she could have thought me capable of doing the deed she had originally accused me of.

"You mean, you saw a woman in the study?" gasped Murray.

"We — ell, a person, rather," she conceded. "The silhouette of someone leaning over the desk. I only had a quick glimpse. I told the policeman I couldn't really say if it was a man or a woman, or what they were wearing."

"Was the study badly damaged?"

"I'm afraid so," said Tim. "It was almost completely gutted. Only a few books on the farthest shelves were able to be salvaged. As for the rest, everything was reduced to ashes!"

"Julie!" Murray turned to me in dismay. "Does that mean all your weeks of work have been in vain? You were so excited when you spoke to me on the telephone yesterday, because you had almost finished Mrs. Briarton's memoirs, and because, from your professional experience, you thought her book would prove a big success!

"My dear!" he looked at me with sympathy in his eyes. "What a tragedy for you, un-less," he added hopefully, "you think you could re-write the whole from memory?"

I uttered a nervous laugh.

"Thank goodness I won't have to do that! I have never been noted for a wonderful memory!

"Fortunately, as it happens, I have a copy of all the notes I made, as well as the carbon copy of the book, which I keep in my own room, so that I can work on the project when I feel like it. I have even got photo-copies of all the diaries there for reference, so you see," I heaved another nervous sigh, "although all the original diaries have been burned, as well as, most unfortunately most of the photographs and news cuttings which were of such help to me, things are not nearly as bad as they might have been!

"Yes!" I assured my listeners, "once Mrs. Briarton is strong enough to give the manu-script the go ahead, I shall send it off to a publisher.

"I am so glad I took the precaution of making these copies," I added. "The publi-cation of her book will give Liz something to look forward to. Something to live for!"

Fortunately as I spoke these words, I had no idea what was in store for me before Liz's dream was realised.

TWELVE

Pino's loud exclamation of delight at my news reminded us that he and Angelina were still in the room.

Rather sharply, Tim turned to them and said, "That will be all for now, thanks, Pino. Angelina, would you please check that Nurse Campbell has everything she needs."

Morag grimaced at Tim after the two Italians had left the room.

"Angelina's ears flap all the time, don't they?" she observed. "I wager she knows more of what goes on in this house than anyone else! She always seems to be there or thereabouts when things happen, and she has more curiosity than any cat!"

"It's a pity her curiosity didn't make her take a closer look to see what was going on in the study last night," muttered Tim. "If she had, she might have frightened the intruder away before he had time to start the fire."

"No!" I shuddered. "If he had seen her, he might have assaulted her before she could summon help. A man like that, who would set fire to a house out of mischief, even although he must have known there were people asleep in the building, would not have treated anyone who got in his way gently! I'm glad she thought it was me who was in there, and didn't poke her nose in to see what I was up to!"

"Let's talk of something else," said Morag quickly. "It gives me the creeps to think there's a maniac like that abroad in the neighbourhood. I'll have to tell Roberto and the rest of the staff to be on the look out, and to make doubly certain all the doors and windows in all the annexes, as well as in the main building are safely secured at night. A fire at the Centre could ruin us!"

The clock on the mantelpiece chimed.

Morag looked at it with disbelief.

"Surely it isn't half past three already! I'll have to fly! I'm expecting a man to call about the new heating system in half an hour."

Tim accompanied her to the front door, and as they were leaving the room, I heard him say, "Morag, about tonight —"

What was to happen tonight I didn't learn because Murray came over to sit on the arm of my chair and smile down at me, saying,

"My poor Julie! What a time you must have had last night! Still, it's a blessing the fire didn't take a firm hold or things could have been so much worse."

"They're bad enough as it is." I sighed. "What with Liz so ill, and most of her prized photographs and souvenirs burned in the study.

"It doesn't seem fair," I shook my head. "Just when things seemed on the turn for her, why should this happen to her?"

"Some people seem to get a rub of bad luck," said Murray. "Still, it's usually followed by a spell of good luck, so maybe only nice things will happen to Mrs. Briarton from now on!"

"I wonder! Nothing ever seems to have gone right for the Richmonds," I pointed out. "It's been bad luck all the way for them for years!"

"That reminds me!" Murray stood up. "In all the excitement, I almost forgot the purpose of my visit! I'd better make tracks to Janey's grandparents as soon as possible. There will be a great many things to discuss, and a great many papers to sign —" he stopped short.

"Damn!" he muttered. "It's going to be much more complicated now!

"You see, Mrs. Briarton is a trustee," he told me what Liz had earlier told me herself. "If she is too ill to sign the necessary papers," he breathed in through his teeth in a worried manner, "this business is going to take a great deal more time than I had anticipated!

"Still," he added hopefully, "Possibly by tomorrow Mrs. Brairton will be sitting up and taking notice, so my best bet is to get on with what I can get on with, and have all the papers ready for her to sign the minute she's able to."

"What if she's ill for some time?"

"We'll cross that bridge when we come to it. In any case, to expedite the child's getting to Switzerland as quickly as possible, I have already arranged with my bank manager to advance me a personal loan, which I shall offer the Richmonds. He knows I've plenty of security behind me, in spite of his usual hummings and hawings before he agreed!

"Now, I'll be on my way, Julie. The sooner I go, the sooner I shall be back to take you out for that promised dinner!"

He strode from the room, and I crossed to the window to watch him get into his

Porsche and go speeding down the drive. In no time at all, at the rate he was going, he would catch up on Morag, whose car I had heard start up only seconds before Murray had left me.

Tim sauntered back into the living room and poured himself out a fresh cup of coffee.

"I take it Murray has gone off to visit the Richmonds?"

I nodded.

"He's in a hurry to get everything settled as quickly as possible."

"It was good of him to come all this way to expedite matters. A bit out of character, I thought at first, but then, perhaps there is another reason why he wanted to come to Ardcraig?" Tim eyed me quizzically.

I refused to be drawn, and after seconds of silence he asked, "What are you doing with yourself this afternoon, Julie? I don't expect you are in the mood to return to work on Liz's book."

"There's actually very little I can do about it now, until she has read it over herself, to decide if she likes the way I have written it," I replied. "So," I continued, "I thought I might help Pino in the garden."

"I have a better idea!" he smiled. "I have books of material samples over at the farm,

200

and I would be grateful if you would look through them, and chose curtains for me for the various rooms in the house.

"Interior decorating is not my forte, any more than it is Morag's, as you can tell from the décor at the Centre!" he grinned.

"I don't know if I should go out and leave Liz," I demurred.

"The nurse is with her, and Angelina is also on duty. If you are wanted, they can 'phone to you at the farm."

"Well, if you're sure you want me to come," I was still hesitant.

"Yes, please!" he smiled coaxingly.

"In that case," I couldn't help smiling back at him, "I really would like to go with you. I've been dying to see the inside of your farm for weeks, it looks so attractive from the outside!"

"Good! I shall go and tell Angelina where she can get in touch with you, and also tell her that there will be four of us for dinner tonight, not to mention the nurse.

"I asked Morag if she would like to join us, since Murray was staying at Matfield."

I knew Murray had mentioned that he was going to take me out to dinner at some distant hotel that evening, but Tim's suggestion appealed to me much more. For one thing, I didn't want to go too far away from

Matfield when Liz was so ill. For another, since my second meeting with him, I hadn't felt quite so much attracted to Murray. Compared with Tim, he seemed too conscious of his charm, too sure of himself.

Moreover, when Morag had been in the room, I had noticed how often they glanced surreptitiously at each other, and I suspected that they still had an affection, one for the other, which their pride would not let them openly admit.

Tim moved towards the door.

"I'll meet you at the front in five minutes," he proposed, "but before you join me there," his smiling glance rested on the pretty high heeled sandals I was wearing, "I advise you to put on more sensible shoes! Those ones aren't quite the thing for walking over farm land!"

When he had gone, I hurried up to Mrs. Briarton's room, to ask the nurse if her patient showed any signs of improvement.

"She hasn't opened her eyes since I arrived, Miss Gilbert," she said, "but her breathing seems a lot easier. I am sure if she can hold her own overnight, she will pull through!"

The nurse's cheering words made me feel more light-hearted as I hurried downstairs to join Tim and gave him the latest bulletin on Liz's condition.

We strolled together down the drive, making for the short cut through the spinney and the water meadow which bordered the Home Farm fields.

The storm had blown itself out with the dawn, and now it was a glorious afternoon — one of those perfect early summer days when the sky is cloudless, the sun bathes everything in golden light, and the balmy west coast air is soft as a caress on the cheeks.

The new, light green of the larches, the blazing yellow of the drifts of broom on the hillside, the heavily scented white may blossoms which weighed down the hedgerows much as the winter snow had weighed them down earlier in the year, and the drifts of mauve lady's smock, interspersed with buttercups and daisies and early marguerites, made an idyllic picture as we walked leisurely towards our destination, shielding our eyes from time to time from the brilliant reflection of the calm waters of the loch which lapped the shores on either side of the arm of land on which Matfield had been built.

The Home Farm itself wasn't built on the peninsula, but nestled in the shelter of the mountain slopes where the neck broadened out.

The white-washed building was further sheltered from the north winds by a circle of tall trees under which soft green foliage, torn from the branches by the previous night's gale, lay like a carpet spread out to welcome us.

It was a low building, with attic windows jutting boldly from below steeply sloping slates. All the windows were framed by climbing roses not yet in bloom, and early honeysuckle whose perfume sweetened the air. The view from those windows, down the long arm of the loch to the open sea beyond, must be breath-taking, I thought, as I eagerly entered the house.

Inside, the woodwork had been stripped of paint to reveal the loveliness of the original pine, and white painted walls gave the low-ceilinged rooms an airiness and lightness.

"There's still a lot to be done," confessed Tim. "The bathroom and kitchen are complete, though," he added proudly, taking me into the largest room in the farm, a kitchen-dining room, which might have been the original of a photograph from the latest Home and House Magazine, and which any woman would have admired.

"Now that the good weather is with us, I am concentrating on the outside work, and next week, hopefully, the first of the deer will be arriving from Glensaugh. Hinds calve in June, and I want the young deer to be born here, used to captivity."

"Do you think deer farming has a future?" I queried.

"It's been done at Rahoy and Glensaugh, where I am getting most of my stock from, although I am also going to try to get some of the animals from the hills over yonder. We have plenty of them running wild hereabouts, and most of my neighbours will be only too glad if I take them and fence them in, away from their crops!"

He crossed to look out of the window.

"Actually, I was the one who suggested the idea of deer farming to Uncle Charles. It is already an established fact in New Zealand, and the two experimental units in Scotland show it can be done here too.

"At the Invermay Agricultural Station in New Zealand tests have been made, comparing the carcase gain over a period between cattle and deer — I'll not bore you with the details," he added with a smile. "Once I get on my hobby horse, there's no stopping me! All I'll tell you now is that the results show deer production compares very favourably with sheep and cattle, and venison is a highly sought after food.

"I know the initial cost will be high. The cost of building a perimeter six foot high fence and the usual four to five foot internal fence, makes me go hot and cold when I think of it, although fortunately there was quite a lot of fencing already on the farm which I can make use of for my deer unit.

"However, there's still a lot of money to be found to get the place exactly as I want it to be, but I'll just have to forge ahead slowly, frustrating though it may be.

"But you haven't come here to listen to my problems, Julie! Let's go to the living room and I'll show you those books of patterns."

He cupped his hand under my elbow to guide me across the little hall and the touch of his fingers stirred my senses as they had done once before. More than ever I became aware of the compelling attraction this man had for me.

I had always enjoyed his pleasant company, now, at his touch, my pleasure increased. I had a sensation of one-ness with him; a sense of belonging.

The momentary attraction Murray Sheil had held for me had been nothing like this; merely a passing fancy which had proved a pale emotion in comparison to what I felt now.

Afraid lest the warm coursing of my blood through my veins would betray the state of my feelings, I moved away from Tim, to cross to the broad window sill on which the books of sample curtain materials lay.

He followed me, and brushed against my arm as he opened a book.

"Once you have chosen the fabrics for me, Julie," he said, "I shall cajole Angelina into making the curtains for me."

A stupid twinge of jealousy at the mention of the pretty Italian girl's name made me say tartly, "You seem to make a habit of cajoling people into doing things for you, don't you? You get me to choose your curtains, Angelina to make them, why," I said angrily, "you even got the Brigadier to leave you this farm you coveted!"

Tim laughed, not in the least put out.

"Dear Julie!" he slipped an arm round my waist and gave it a light, affectionate squeeze. "What funny ideas you have in that pretty head of yours, and," his own eyes glinted, "what lovely eyes you have when they sparkle like that!"

He removed his clasp from my waist and stepped back from me.

"Believe me," his tone was less teasing

now, "I asked you to come here with me to-day because I wanted to show you my house and because I felt quite sure you would know exactly what kind of curtains to choose for it. I know you have an eye for colours and textures from the clothes you wear. What is more, I rather thought you would enjoy choosing the curtains.

"As for asking Angelina to make them up, to be honest, she offered to do so. You no doubt know she is a very good seamstress and makes all her own clothes, as well as mending the linen at Matfield.

"She genuinely enjoys sewing, she tells me.

"Finally, as to the farm," his lips tightened, "I don't know what stories you have been hearing or who has been telling them to you, but the fact is I inherited the Home Farm because I am the oldest Briarton in the line of succession, and the farm and its land and most of the estate surrounding Matfield is entailed."

"Then why didn't you inherit Matfield?" I was still doubtful.

"That is an involved story. Simply told, it appears that the original Matfield House was burned to the ground at the turn of the nineteenth century. The present house wasn't rebuilt on the same spot. It wasn't even built on Briarton land, but on land belonging to a neighbour whose daughter married the then head of the Brairton family. Somehow the new house and its land was never legally added to the entail, although this wasn't discovered until the Brigadier was going over some old family documents.

"He brought the matter to old Mr. Sheil's notice, to make sure it would be in order for him to leave his wife the house, should he predecease her.

"I'm glad he did, mainly because it would have been unfair to turn Liz out of the house in which she had lived for so long, but also," he added with a twinkle, "I couldn't possibly afford to keep up a place the size of Matfield!

"At least Liz can afford to do that!"

I couldn't say anything. Inside me, relief was bubbling up, choking me. I was so happy to know I had been right in my estimation of Tim. He wasn't a sycophant, who had toadied to an old man to get what he wanted from him. He hadn't done Liz out of anything which should have been hers.

To conceal what I was feeling, I bent swiftly over the book of patterns and flicked through the samples.

"While you are looking through the books, Julie, I'll take the Land Rover from the shed and make a tour of the fences, to see if any of the uprights have been loosened by last night's gale," said Tim. "I won't be long."

I went to the window to wave goodbye to him, then spent a pleasant half hour, wandering through the house, imagining what the rooms would look like with such and such curtains hanging at the windows.

I even thought of the carpets I would choose to cover the bare floor boards and the kind of furniture with which I would fill the rooms.

A pine dresser would fit well into the dining section of the kitchen and show off the willow pattern plates I had inherited from my grandmother. I would have a comfortable suite in the living room, upholstered to match the curtains I had chosen for it, and I would have book shelves on either side of the fireplace.

I would have —

I stopped short. I was being a fool, daydreaming like this!

I was picturing this farmhouse as I would like to see it, because I felt I belonged here. I could even picture myself happily settled here, with Tim, and our children.

The strength of feeling which swept

through me with these futile thoughts, frightened me.

I knew that now, for the first time in my life, I was in love — truly, deeply in love!

The tragedy of it was that the man who roused those deep feelings in me was not mine to love. He was in love with someone else. With a woman I did not think loved him in return.

THIRTEEN

Tim insisted on brewing up a cup of tea for me before we returned to Matfield.

"You are the first person who has shared a cup here with me," he smiled. "I hope it won't be the last time you visit me, and share a cuppa either!"

I turned away from him, so that he wouldn't see the sudden quivering of my lips.

"It could be. I shall be leaving Matfield soon, you know. My contract finishes in the middle of June, and since the book is finished, there is no need for Liz to keep me on.

"If she wants me to revise it later, or help her out with any difficulties which may arise, she can write to me."

"Haven't you been happy here?" he asked anxiously. "From your tone, I gather you are glad at the thought of leaving us."

"I have been very happy here!" I said

quickly. "Until now, that is. What happened last night changed things. I don't think anything will be quite the same again.

"The doctor is even afraid that if Liz does recover, she may not be able to walk, or even to speak. The shock has affected her vocal nerves, or so he fears. Even if I stayed on, what would there be for me to do? I'm not a nurse."

"Liz loves you, Julie. It would be a comfort for her to know that you were still around. Couldn't you stay on, Julie?" he pleaded. "Even if there isn't enough work to keep you busy, you could always get down to writing that book of your own you keep telling me about — the novel of the century?"

He continued to look at me coaxingly.

"Liz would never find anyone else like you to act as companion."

"I'm not a companion help, Tim. You know what my work is! I wish I could stay here, but I simply can't afford to!"

"You would have your salary, and your keep. No rent to pay. No extras to spend your money on. Isn't that enough for you?" he sounded angry.

"Tim, you don't understand!" I cried. "I know I shouldn't tell you this, but I don't see that it matters now. Liz is broke! She couldn't afford to pay me anything, once my contract is up! All she has is her pension and a small annuity, which will scarcely cover Pino's and Angelina's wages! That's why she had this idea of writing her memoirs! She thought — in fact — she knew, she would make money from them, although last night," I bit my lip, "something she said made me wonder if she was getting cold feet about her revelations."

Tim was looking at me so oddly, I felt I had to explain further.

"You see, Liz hasn't always been the kind of person she was after she married the Brigadier and came to live here! Your great uncle even didn't know the truth about her. That she was the talk of the town. That her name was notorious in the twenties and thirties.

"Tim, some of the scandals she reveals in her memoirs will shock you and her friends and neighbours — if she does decide to publish — as she possibly will finally decide to do, to restore the wing that was destroyed."

"I still don't understand why she has to write her memoirs to make money," said Tim, in a tone of voice which told me he hadn't fully taken in what I had been telling him about Liz's past.

"The Brigadier left her a wealthy woman,"

214

he persisted. "A very wealthy woman!"

"No!" I shook my head. "That's what everyone thinks, but Murray told me the truth, and Liz herself also confided in me.

"Her husband left her Matfield, and a death-bed promise not to sell it but to keep it in the way it had always been kept, like a show place!

"His pensions and his annuities had died with him. What capital he had had, had been used to keep Matfield going during his lifetime. Now there was next to nothing left!

"Liz was much too proud to tell people that her husband hadn't been as well off as they had presumed him to be. Possibly she thought she would be letting him down if she did, so she determined by her own efforts to make money to keep her promise to him!"

Tim gulped down his tea.

"I'm sorry to rush you, Julie," he said abruptly, "but I have just realised that there is someone I must get in touch with before he leaves his office. I'll take the Land Rover to get to Ardcraig, and I'll drop you off at Matfield."

He practically ran me out to the yard and pushed me up into the vehicle which was standing there. He didn't once open his mouth during the short, fast run to Matfield, but he did at least take time to lift me down from the Land Rover when we got there, saying, as he held me in his arms for a brief moment.

"I may be gone some time, Julie. Tell Angelina to serve dinner an hour later than usual, will you please?"

He clambered up behind the driving wheel and drove away, leaving me standing in front of the house, wondering what had caused his sudden change of plans, for I was sure he had originally intended to spend the whole afternoon with me.

When Murray returned to the house half an hour later from his visit to the Richmonds, I told him I didn't want to go out that evening, in case Liz took another bad turn.

I thought it more tactful to put the change of plan this way, than to tell him I preferred to stay at Matfield and make up a four with Morag and Tim.

To my relief he was quite amenable to the change.

"That suits me, Julie. It will give me more time to study the notes I made this afternoon, and to read over the documents once again in regard to what we discussed.

"I must also get to Ardcraig to catch the

evening mail," he added.

I went up to Liz's room, to ask Nurse Campbell how her patient was.

"She is a bit brighter. She's speaking more clearly now," said the nurse, coming out into the hall to talk to me. "She has been asking for you a lot. She keeps going on about some book. I think perhaps you could go in and see her. It might stop her worrying about whatever it is she has on her mind."

Mrs. Briarton's eyes lit up as I approached her bed, but she looked so small and fragile lying there, I felt like weeping, and it was an effort to force a smile.

"You had us worried, Liz! I'm glad to see you look so much better!"

"I feel so weak!" she whispered. "I thought I would die when I saw the fire engines, and thought Matfield was on fire!"

"It was only a little fire. There was no great damage done."

"My book? How about my book. They said the study was burned —"

"Your book is safe, Liz. It's finished and ready for you to O.K. it!"

"Julie, I'm so tired," her eyelids fluttered shut, and she opened them again with difficulty. "So tired," she repeated. "I haven't the strength to read — to think —"

She put her hand out to take hold of mine.

217

"I'm going to leave the final decision to you. I would like you to send the manuscript away as quickly as possible, if you are satisfied with it!"

"But —"

"Please, Julie. No arguments. I don't want to make decisions. I'm so tired. Please do as I say. Send it. Send it," her voice slurred over and her eyelids closed again.

"The pills make her drowsy," explained Nurse Campbell. "I think you should leave us now. Sleep is the best thing for her. Don't look so worried, lass," she went on. "If Mrs. Briarton doesn't get worked up about anything, there is no reason why she shouldn't pull through."

I couldn't help worrying as I went to my rooms and listlessly got ready for the little dinner party. Liz's condition, my own hopeless feelings for Tim, subdued my natural joie de vivre. I wasn't even interested in what I would wear, although last night, looking forward to Murray's arrival, I had spent some time wondering what to put on for our date.

I chose a sombre dress to suit my mood; a high-necked, long sleeved gown of deep midnight blue velvet, pinning a marcasite lizard to the mandarin collar to relieve the starkness and pushing a marcasite and pearl dress ring on my finger.

The dark colour of the dress seemed to deepen the colour of my eyes, making them seem enormous.

I had let my hair grow during my stay at Matfield, and now it was below shoulder length, and its gleaming bracken-brown showed up well against the dark fabric.

I was putting the finishing touches to my make-up when I saw Morag's car come up the drive. I knew Tim wasn't back yet, which meant I would have to entertain his friend. She was very early, I thought, until I remembered that Tim had probably forgotten to tell her of the change of the dinner hour.

Angelina was showing her into the dining room by the time I reached the hall, and as I crossed towards her, I thought how stunning she looked tonight.

She was wearing a flame-coloured dress, with a low plunging neckline. Gold hoop earrings dangled from her tiny lobes and a gold necklet in the form of a snake with a malevolent green eye encircled her throat.

She looked dressed to kill for such an informal party and I found myself wondering who her prey would be tonight. Tim, it should be, but being Morag she might have decided to amuse herself with her ex-fiancé. I hadn't been oblivious to the oblique glances she had directed at him when he had arrived at Matfield that afternoon, and it was possible she still secretly regretted breaking her engagement with the attractive and successful young lawyer.

I felt somewhat self-conscious playing the part of hostess to the girl who might sooner than anyone had expected, herself become the hostess of Matfield.

Everyone expected that Tim would inherit the place from Liz, and that might be part of the attraction he had for the lovely, ambitious girl to whom I was handing a glass of sherry.

Morag was in an amiable mood. She chattered non-stop about her forthcoming holiday to the Italian Dolomites, where she as going to stay at one of the premier resorts in a hotel owned by Roberto's father.

"He is going to teach me some of the tricks of the hotel trade!" she told me. "While I have been able to cope with the sports side of our venture, neither my brother nor I know much about the catering side, and I'm told this is where money can be made or lost!

"Roberto's father has been in the business all his life, and I should learn a lot from him. My holiday will be a mixture of business and pleasure!"

Tim arrived as we were discussing the holiday, and poured himself a sherry.

"Where is Murray?" he demanded. "It's almost dinner time, and Angelina won't be pleased if there is a further delay."

"Maybe he has fallen asleep?" suggested Morag. "I shall go and bang on the dinner gong in the hall. That will rouse him!"

"No!" said Tim hastily. "That would disturb Liz! I'll go and knock on his door."

Murray, who had been looking somewhat tense and worried when he had gone up to his room, still looked as if he had something on his mind.

"What's the matter with you?" demanded Morag. "You don't look in the best of humours! Are Janey's affairs keeping you from dating a beautiful blonde in Edinburgh tonight?" she teased him.

"Edinburgh couldn't provide a prettier brunette or a prettier blonde than the ones I'm dining with here!" he retorted with a flash of his usual flattery.

Tim didn't seem amused by his retort, but Morag said, smiling, "Save your blarney for your old ladies, Murray. It cuts no ice here!"

I handed him a glass of sherry and he

smiled down at me before replying to Morag.

"I'm not the only one who flatters old ladies, or old men for that matter," he added. "Some of us are even better at it, to their own advantage, than I am!"

His eyes strayed briefly to Tim, and I thought, Why! He's jealous of Tim! He's annoyed because he thinks Tim has taken Morag away from him!

Morag laughed, as if she too guessed what was in Murray's mind.

"I wouldn't thank anyone for leaving me a place like this! It would be a millstone round one's neck. It would cost a fortune to convert to a hotel. The rooms are all the wrong size, and no one in their senses would want a private house this size nowadays.

"Looking at it from a practical point of view, it's rather a pity it wasn't burned to the ground in last night's fire. The insurance money would be a lot better than all the bricks and mortar!"

"Morag!" I gasped, outraged. "How can you say such a thing!"

"Because it's true," she challenged me. "You have to be practical these days, Julie. Keeping up a place this size would just soak up money like a sponge. I would rather have the hard cash any day, and when it came to the nitty gritty, I'll bet the same would go for all of you!" she tossed her head, so that the gold earrings flashed like darts of lightning in the glow from the overhead lamp.

"And talking of cash, I wouldn't mind having a little of the commodity at this moment. I've ordered some bathing huts, and I'm having the boat shed repaired, and the jetty in our private bay extended, and my bank manager isn't being at all co-operative about a loan!"

"The trouble with you, Morag," observed Murray knowingly, "is that your ideas have always been too big for your bank balance. One day you will land yourself in trouble!"

She pouted at him.

"You would never let that happen, darling, would you?" she put her hand on his arm and looked up at him with her enchantress's eyes. "You would bail me out, wouldn't you, if the worse came to the worst. Not that that's likely now!" she added with a sly gleam in her eyes. "I do know where I can always get a sponsor!"

Tim's lips tightened at the way she was teasing Murray.

"It's time we went in for dinner," he said sharply. "And for heaven's sake, let's talk of something other than money. I am sick to death of the subject!"

He grabbed my arm and propelled me so roughly towards the dining room, I was sure the flesh of my forearm would be bruised.

"How is Mrs. Briarton this evening?" Murray switched the conversation smoothly once we were seated at table.

"She seems to be a little better," I replied, equally glad, as Tim was, to get away from the subject of Matfield and the money required to maintain it.

I still had guilty twinges about betraying Liz's secret to Tim, and wished, now, I had said nothing.

"She is even beginning to take an interest in things," I went on brightly. "Do you know, she is insisting that I send her book off to the publisher without further delay, although she hasn't read the manuscript! She says if I think it is good enough, that's enough recommendation!"

"And will you send it?" asked Morag.

"I don't know. I would prefer her to have a look at it, and yet, in her present state of health, she might get over upset if I didn't do what she asked me to.

"I'll sleep on it," I decided, spreading some of the delectable terrine which Angelina had served as first course on a piece of toast.

The young housekeeper had excelled herself tonight with the meal she had prepared for us, and even Murray was so impressed with the menu that he said he was glad we had decided to dine at Matfield instead of making a round journey of some forty miles to the hotel he had intended taking me.

"I don't suppose I could tempt you away from Matfield to come and cater for me at the Sports Centre?" Morag asked Angelina when she was serving coffee in the lounge after the meal. "I could do with someone like you.

"On the other hand, I don't suppose you will be staying on at Matfield much longer in any case. I have an idea that that young man of yours is wanting to whisk you off with him!"

Her last remarks made Angelina blush, but she said nothing.

I didn't share everyone else's high opinion of Angelina when later that night I went up to my bedroom and noticed that several things weren't as I had left them.

Papers on the table I used as a work desk had been disturbed, and the locked suitcase under my bed in which I had put the diaries and the manuscript for safe keeping had been moved, so that I could not reach it.

I felt my hackles rise with anger. Angelina had never let her curiosity drive her to such lengths before, and her action troubled me.

If anything happened to these precious papers now, it would be a tragedy. I didn't want the responsibility of having them in my possession any longer.

First thing in the morning, or at any rate as soon as I was free to do so, I would take the diaries to the bank for safe keeping.

As for the book, I would spend the morning giving it a final going over for any minor faults I may have overlooked in my previous revisions, and then I would do as Mrs. Briarton had asked me.

I would send it to my publisher friend and leave it to him if he wanted any further changes. He would also know, better than I would, if we should get a legal expert to read it in order to make sure that Liz hadn't laid herself open to any court actions by some of the things she was revealing to the public.

I felt so relieved when I made this decision, that no sooner had my head touched the pillow, than I fell into a deep, restful sleep.

FOURTEEN

Tim had gone off early to Inverness on urgent business, and I was sorry I hadn't seen him before he left, because I had wanted to tell him the decision I had come to about Liz's book.

I also missed his cheerful company at breakfast, because Murray, who came to table when I was about half way through the meal, didn't look in the best of moods, and sat glowering at the plate in front of him, making no attempt at conversation.

However, when I was pouring out my final cup of coffee I decided to break the strained silence.

"Murray," I announced, "I have decided to do what Mrs. Briarton asked. I am giving her book a final check over this morning, and then I shall post it off to the publisher this afternoon!"

He looked across at me and smiled unexpectedly.

"I think you are doing the right thing, Julie. You might have upset Mrs. Brairton if you hadn't complied with her wishes."

"What time are you returning to Edinburgh?" I asked.

"I've decided to stay one more day," he continued to smile at me, as if he had got over his morning blues and was switching on his charm again. "I didn't expect you would have any work to do, and I thought it would be nice to spend the day together. However, at least we can go for a drive in the afternoon, can't we? There is a pleasant little hotel I know not too far away where we could have afternoon tea."

He was taking my acceptance of his invitation for granted, but I decided not to argue the point. It would be churlish to turn him down when he was making an effort to be friendly.

"We shall have to stop at Ardcraig on the way," I said. "I want to post the manuscript and I also want to put the copies of the diaries into the bank for safe keeping."

"That's an excellent idea!" he approved enthusiastically. "I should have thought of it!"

After lunch, served early because it was Angelina's afternoon off duty, Murray and I set off down the drive in his Porsche.

To my annoyance, instead of going direct to the village, he turned off the main road into the steep and twisting but picturesque road which led over Ardcraig Pass.

"Murray!" I protested. "I told you I wanted to post my parcel in Ardcraig, and also to go to the bank. This is early closing day!"

"We've plenty of time," he assured me. "I want to take a photograph of Ardcraig Castle from the viewpoint up here, when the sun is in its present position, and then I'll drive you to the Post Office."

"You could have taken a photograph from the shore road," I grumbled.

"Everyone takes one from there. I want something different!"

"You like being different, don't you? You like doing things with style."

"Why not. I'd hate to be considered 'the man in the street'!" he sneered. "Life has to have style to be enjoyable!"

We went speeding up the winding road, taking the corners so quickly I found myself gripping onto my seat. I wanted to snap at him that we weren't taking part in a motor rally but decided he was possibly hurrying for my sake, so I said nothing.

We stopped at the parking place at the highest part of the road over the Pass. Murray grabbed his camera from the back of the car and turned to me, smiling.

"Out you get, Julie! I want to take a photograph of you too!"

He went scrambling ahead of me up the steep path which led from the parking place to the top of the ridge some fifty feet above.

"Hurry, Julie," he called back to me. "We don't want to waste time!"

My high heeled shoes, which I had put on because I had thought we were going for a drive and not a mountaineering expedition, slipped and slithered on the steep gradient. In no time Murray was out of sight behind the huge boulder which marked the sharp turn round the side of the slope before it opened out to the narrow plateau where the viewfinder had been erected.

I paused for breath and gazed about me. On my left the mountain plunged almost sheerly down to the rocky shore of the loch. High on my right, slopes covered with broom and bracken reared up to the topmost ridge. Below me, I could see the road we had traversed snaking down to join the coast road, where several cars were speeding. Only one car was visible on the col road, climbing up towards us. Even from this distance I recognised Dave Finlay's yellow, open top sports coupé, and had no doubt that the woman in the vivid green blouse who sat beside him was Angelina.

These two had been constant companions for the past three weeks. I wondered what Roberto, if he wasn't too occupied flirting with Morag, thought of this friendship.

"Julie! Do hurry!" Murray called again.

Reluctantly I resumed the climb. I was out of breath by the time I reached the little plateau, and leaned against the pillar of the view indicator, which marked out each mountain top and island and loch which could be seen from this spot.

We were very high up, and looking down at the loch from this height made me feel quite dizzy.

"I've snapped the Castle, now it is your turn!" Murray trained his camera on me.

"Darling," he wheedled. "Do stop clutching at the post and move over to the right a little. A step nearer the edge, so that I can get a better background. Yes, now look down and point to the Castle on the shore. No. That's not right. Take another step forward."

"Is this all right?" I turned to ask him, but almost before the words were out of my mouth I felt his hands on the small of my back, pushing at me.

Just in time I managed to grab at him, and clung to him, trying to retain my balance, and all the while screaming at him, asking him what he was up to.

He tried to force me from him, over the side, but I clung to him like a limpet, realising this was my only chance to save myself, and wondering, all the time, what madness had got in to him.

As we swayed there together, my high heels slipped on the gritty surface and in desperation, fearing I was about to go over the edge, I found unexpected strength to give him a violent shove which sent him reeling back, momentarily loosening his grip of me.

I pulled myself free and reeled away from him, but he came laughing back at me.

I kicked out wildly and the pointed heels of my shoes cracked against his shin bone, then his ankle bone, stopping him in his tracks.

He shouted with pain, hopping on one foot with agony, giving me time to get away from him.

He screamed obscenities after me, then came slithering and running in my wake, trying to catch me once more as I fled down the path towards the roadway.

I was praying that Dave Finlay's car hadn't yet passed this point; praying that someone would help save me from the madman who pursued me.

I had just reached the far side of the road, the side away from the cliff edge, when I tripped and fell. In seconds Murray had caught up with me. He bent down and grabbed me by the hair, then by the arms, dragging me back across the road in spite of my continued struggles, towards the precipitous edge.

I could feel my strength failing. I grew weak with terror. There seemed nothing I could do to save myself. Even my screams sounded fainter in my ears. I closed my eyes, not wanting to see over the brink of the road, not wanting to see death itself, come nearer.

There was a screech of brakes, angry shouts, hysterical screams.

Unexpectedly Murray's hold on me was loosened and at the same time I heard an unprintable oath as Dave Finlay dragged my assailant from me.

Next moment Angelina's arms were round me, comforting me, and her excited voice cried.

"It's all right, Signorina. It's all right. Dave is taking care of the madman. He won't harm you any more!"

Much later that day, after Murray had been arrested and I had been taken to the local hospital for a check up, and the police had asked me a multitude of questions at the police station, I returned to Matfield, but it wasn't until late in the evening, when Tim came back home, that I learned the whys and wherefores of Murray's murderous attack.

We were gathered in the living room — Morag, and Tim, and Mr. Ogilvie from Inverness, who had worked in partnership with old Mr. Sheil, and Dave Finlay and myself. Angelina and Pino were there too, serving coffee, while I sat on the settee with Tim holding my hand, while he told the story.

From boyhood, Murray Sheil had had grandiose ideas. He had always demanded the best of everything. He wanted to be rich and famous: to live a life of luxury. When his dream of becoming a champion racing driver had been thwarted by lack of funds, he determined that never again would he be short of money to do the things that he wanted to do.

Although he made a comfortable living as a lawyer, it wasn't enough to provide him with the luxuries he wanted, and it wasn't long before his cunning mind saw how he could get extra money.

Many of his clients, mainly the ones he had inherited from his father's practice in

Ardcraig, were elderly, and relied on him for advice and guidance in their affairs. It was easy for him to charm them into signing papers for him, papers which gave him control over their assets, which he realised from time to time for his own benefit. He was clever enough not to take too much at a time; clever enough not to take too much from anyone who had a direct heir who might question the transactions.

Brigadier Briarton's affairs seemed tailor made for him. As he grew older, he left the management of his money affairs and of his tax problems to Murray. He had such a good income from his Service pension and other pensions and an annuity, that he had no need to realise any of his considerable capital, for apart from Matfield, he had few expenses.

The old man had no direct heir, only his equally old wife to leave his money to, and Murray was sure if the Brigadier predeceased her, he would be able to explain any discrepancies, to an unworldly octogenarian.

He boldly forged the old man's shakey signature and realised most of his assets, buying for himself with the proceeds a luxury flat in Edinburgh and a smaller flat in Monte Carlo, where he went each year on holiday.

When the Brigadier died he convinced Liz that her husband had used up his capital to maintain Matfield, for she had had no idea how rich he had been. However, it wasn't so easy to convince her she would have to sell her home, and he was worried in case Tim, who was now resident with her, might have had some idea of the extent of his great uncle's wealth, and pose awkward questions if Liz started economising in the upkeep of the place. He even started rumours that Tim was a bit of a sponger, and not to be trusted, so that no one would pay any attention to him if he started poking his nose into Liz's affairs.

Having spent the Brigadier's capital, Murray found himself with nothing to fall back on when he got heavily into debt with his bookmaker. He couldn't let it be known he was hard up, so he decided to borrow from another of his clients, and this time it was the Scott Trust which came in for his attention.

Janey wouldn't get the capital until she was twenty-five, more than a dozen years away, by which time, surely he would have repaid by other means the money he "borrowed."

Now his luck ran out. He was flung into a

panic when Janey became ill and her grand-parents raised the question of getting some capital from the trust to pay for the treatment which the girl so urgently needed. They talked of bringing in their own lawyer should difficulties arise, and Murray could see his dream world collapse if this happened.

He was at his wit's end, wondering how he could talk his way out, or how he could pay the money he had taken back into the fund before the discrepancy was discovered, when I came up with a possible solution!

On the 'phone I told him of Liz's amazing diaries and how, if they fell into a blackmailer's hands, they could make him a fortune.

He decided to have a look at them and that same night he drove to Matfield, broke into the study, forced open the desk and glanced through the diaries. Immediately he realised he held a gold mine in his hands! The man whose name Liz had refused to allow me to mention in the memoirs would alone have provided a blackmailer with a steady income from his massive fortune in order to keep secret his parentage!

Murray felt on top of the world again. In a short time money would come pouring to him. He would be able to put back what he had taken from Janey's capital, but in the meantime he would do as he had intended to do in order to procrastinate the discovery of the deficit — he would offer the Richmonds money to pay for Janey's immediate expenses.

One thing, however, had still to be attended to. He must make sure that none of his victims had the slightest idea of the source of the knowledge he had acquired. Liz's book and the revelation that Elizabeth Thomis was still alive, must be kept from the public!

A fire, which he hoped would be attributed to an electric fault, would destroy the manuscript, the notes, the newscuttings — everything except the diaries, which would himself keep. He piled the papers loosely round the desk, together with every bit of flammable material he could lay hands on, and set them alight. He waited until he was sure the papers had been destroyed before he escaped from the room. He hoped the blaze would spread to the rest of the house, for the shock might kill Mrs. Briarton. Her death would add to his feeling of security.

He drove back to Edinburgh and was in his office at his usual time in the morning. There he sent off his blackmailing letters before driving north once again to keep his appointment with the Richmonds.

I shattered his sense of well-being by telling him I still had copies of the diaries and of the book, and that Liz had demanded that I send the manuscript to the publisher forthwith!

He was in a tight corner and he had to act quickly. I mustn't be allowed to send off the book, and the copies must be destroyed! But how?

I seemed to hand him his answer on a plate when I asked him to take me to Ardcraig in the afternoon not only to post the book, but to deposit the diaries in the bank!

Now all he had to do was to arrange for a fatal accident to me en route, get hold of the documents, and that was that. My death might even prove the final shock for Liz's frail constitution, and then all the loose ends would be cleared up!

Fortunately for me his plan miscarried and now he would have to pay for his felonies!

We determined to keep the news of Murray's activities from Liz until she was strong enough to cope with the situation.

"You will stay on here now, won't you, Julie, until Liz is well again?" pleaded Tim. "Treat your stay as a holiday. It will only be for a week or two, and Liz will be glad to know you are near at hand."

I sighed drearily and crossed to look out of the window.

How could I stay here, under the same roof as Tim, loving him as I did, without betraying my feelings? His very kindness to me and the affectionate regard with which he treated me, made things too difficult.

"Please stay, Signorina Gilbert!" Pino added his plea, and Angelina nodded agreement.

I looked at the five people who were watching me hopefully, for even Morag and Dave seemed to want me to stay. Only the lawyer, whom I had met for the first time that day, didn't add his voice to the others.

Tim came over to stand beside me and slipped his arm round my waist.

"You belong here, Julie," he said softly. "Matfield wouldn't be the same without you. It needs you!"

I wasn't aware that the others had quietly left the room and that we were alone together.

I was only aware that Tim was looking at me in a way which made me shiver with emotion, and that his clasp round my waist was growing firmer.

"Morag might resent me," I tried to pull away.

"What's Morag got to do with it?" he seemed genuinely surprised.

"I thought that you and she —" I stuttered to a halt.

Tim laughed.

"Morag and I are friendly sparring partners, that's all! I'm not her kind of man! No, she will be very happy with Roberto, who adores her, and who will let her dominate him, and who will help her with her Centre!"

He forced me to look at him.

"Surely you weren't jealous of Morag?" he teased.

My lips quivered.

"I — I thought — I really thought —" I sniffed.

"Darling!" he stared at me, his mouth broadening to a grin. "You were jealous of Morag! You were! That must mean —" he laughed, "Oh, you little idiot! How can you be so blind after all these weeks!"

He took me in his arms and held me so close I could feel his heart beat against me.

"My darling!" his mouth muzzled my ear. "My darling! Surely you must have realised how I felt about you!"

"Tim!" I sighed blissfully, clinging to him.

He kissed my forehead, my eyes, my cheeks.

"You will stay on here, won't you, Julie, for my sake, if not for Liz's?" his smile teased me.

"I didn't want to go!" I smiled back. "I didn't want to leave you!"

He held me at arms' length for a moment, looking at me long and tenderly.

"We shall always stay together. Always, my darling!" he promised. "How I love you, Julie! How I longed to say those very words to you!"

He repeated them as he held me close once more.

"Yes, I do love you, Julie!"

I thought, briefly, how delighted Liz would be. She loved Tim. She loved me. What greater happiness could we give her than the knowledge that we loved each other? No doctor could have prescribed a better tonic for her!

My happiness glowed in my eyes as I looked up at Tim. My love was warm on my lips as I returned his first fierce, lengthy, passionate kiss.

We hope you have enjoyed this Large Print book. Other Thorndike, Wheeler, and Chivers Press Large Print books are available at your library or directly from the publishers.

For information about current and upcoming titles, please call or write, without obligation, to:

Publisher
Thorndike Press
295 Kennedy Memorial Drive
Waterville, ME 04901
Tel. (800) 223-1244

or visit our Web site at:

www.gale.com/thorndike
www.gale.com/wheeler

OR

Chivers Large Print
published by BBC Audiobooks Ltd
St James House, The Square
Lower Bristol Road
Bath BA2 3SB
England
Tel. +44(0) 800 136919
email: bbcaudiobooks@bbc.co.uk
www.bbcaudiobooks.co.uk

All our Large Print titles are designed for easy reading, and all our books are made to last.